T0300621

Ursula Whitcher
NORTH CONTINENT RIBBON

Neon Hemlock Press

Neon Hemlock Press
www.neonhemlock.com
@neonhemlock

North Continent Ribbon
Ursula Whitcher

Cover Illustration by Danielle Taphanel
Interior Illustrations by Matthew Spencer
Cover Design and Layout by dave ring

Print ISBN-13: 978-1-952086-84-7
Ebook ISBN-13: 978-1-952086-85-4

North Continent Ribbon

By Ursula Whitcher

For everyone from The Intolerable Clock, where this all began.

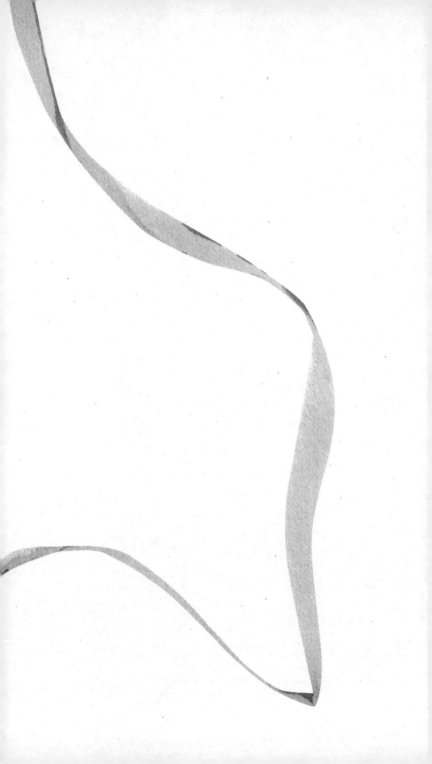

STORIES

FROM CROSS-PLANETARY INVESTMENT: A PRACTICAL VRASELIAN'S GALACTIC OPPORTUNITY HANDBOOK (3RD ED., 538 VRASELE/3381 NAKHORIAN RECKONING):

Best known for shipping conglomerates such as Cypress and Gentian Corp., the planet of **Nakharat** (named for its dominant ethnic group, the Nakhorians) is a major exporter of faster-than-light vehicular components sourced from a high-orbit E-type singularity. Significant exports of planetary origin include bovine and caprine germlines as well as luxury products such as textiles and worked jade. Direct investment is constrained by a complex regulatory environment that places major restrictions on intelligent machine assistance. Most prospective investors will find it easiest to partner with a local corporate interest, though in some cases triangulating via municipal or rural authorities can provide significant benefits. (The latter often use pseudo-military titles such as General or Colonel; investors should not be deterred by these terms, which in the local context primarily indicate agricultural expertise.) Settlement and culture are focused on the major "Western" landmass…

FROM THE WRITINGS OF SAINT NAVYAI (JUVENILIA) (C. 3092 NAKHORIAN RECKONING):

I told him, if you're writing poetry, it's not enough to say one true thing. You have to pack in all the ways of being true, until the words tremble, like a cup that spills when you touch it.

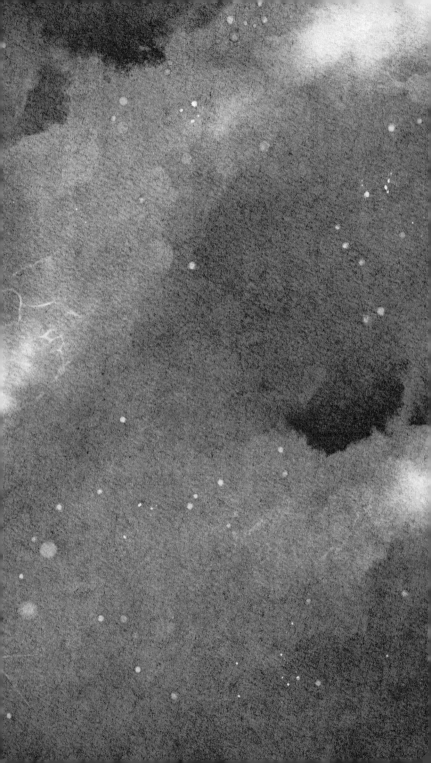

CLOSER THAN YOUR KIDNEYS

in the year 2934 of the Nakhorian reckoning

I MET THE khanym when I tried to kill her. I broke into her office at the core of the hundredship, my sword shining white in my hand.

Yes, I had a glowing sword. Kids who grew up on the plains think a rifle is a warrior's weapon. But you never fire a gun if you're not willing to hit whatever lies behind the target. On a hundredship, that might be the engine's blood, or a bystander in another compartment, or the stretched metal skin between the ship and the Deep. I was an assassin, not a psychopath. I used a sword.

The khanym had two guards. I stabbed the first as I came through the door. By the time I pulled my blade out of her body, the second guard had activated his own sword. He was taller than me; that wasn't a surprise.

I stepped toward him with a hanging parry, crystal chiming as our blades met. That brought my left hand near his hilt. I pressed his wrist back just long enough to raise my sword and strike his face. My arm absorbed the shock of cutting bone. He slumped and fell. No longer my opponent; no longer caught in the current of our dance. The golden ribbon in his hair was streaked with blood.

I turned toward the back of the room, in search of my quarry, and realized a dart was stuck in my right hand. It glittered like a splinter from my blade. I wore no gloves.

There was another dart in the guard's cheek, but he was dead. The points must have been poisoned, because everything was very slow.

"If I die, you die," the khanym said. She was wearing an amber coat, real silk, that shone like the warning light above a door you shouldn't enter. Her unbound hair hung past her waist. The dart gun in her hand was tiny.

I needed to charge her. It would take five steps. I envisioned myself lifting my sword arm, moving. The whole action would be complete between one pulse and the next of the engine's heart.

The khanym's chest rose and fell. She was breathing fast, a pulse entirely different from the engine hum. I hadn't moved. I watched myself ask, "How so?", forming my lips into a circle round the question.

"The dart tips break into shards," the khanym said. "Microscopic; keyed to me. They are already floating through your bloodstream. They will assemble in the artery beside your kidney. If the signal is lost, they'll cut. You'll bleed out fast."

I couldn't map the details of the biotech, not in this state and perhaps not ever, but I knew what blood loss looked like. The gush, the muscles sliding, slow collapse. But there was an obvious catch: the khanym would have alarms. "If you do not die, I also die."

"You have a choice. I can kill your body, or I can kill

your former self." The khanym's smile was small, and certain. "I do need new guards."

I watched her for another strange, stretched moment, her sleeve fluttering in some overactive ventilation current. In one sense, her threat came too late: I had failed to kill her. What good was I, as Ibex Company's blade? My old self was already dead.

I dropped to my knees and thumbed the button hidden in my sword's hilt. The shining blade retracted with a faint smell of burning blood. Its hilt clunked, dead metal, as I set it on the floor.

"Look at me," the khanym said, which was stupid, since I had not been able to stop looking at her. "Do you renounce your former Company?"

I nodded, and when that did not seem to be enough, I said the words: "I, Tashnur, a daughter of Ibex Company, give up all shares and claim upon its resources. Having failed irretrievably in my duties and obligations. With the khanym Orazet as witness."

She stepped toward me then, placing the dart gun in a pocket. Unlike the guards, whose sole allegiance had been to the khanym, I wore my hair covered. She found the pins that held my scarf to my black cap and lifted away both layers, tossing the fabric behind her. She ran her fingers along the ribbons that bound my braids close to my head. They were mostly pewter-colored, the hull-gray of the Company, but there was a narrow golden lace for the Academy history club—I'd loved the sweep and flow of ancient battles—and a green rayon cord.

"A lover?" she asked.

"Once. We make much better friends." Beylik was a pleasant person. He liked battles in theory, but in practice he was content to do his job, modeling the currents of the Deep around star systems we might never even visit, and wait for minor recognitions. He would raise whatever child the Company gave to him, in time.

I had wanted posterity, a lineage, a daughter whose
name would be followed by my own. Instead I knelt before
the khanym as she cut away every symbol of achievement
I had earned. Her knife was small, its blade crystal-sharp.
I felt the tickle of lost strands against my neck. My head
was far too light.

When all my braids had fallen to the floor, the khanym
tilted my face toward hers. Her brows were long and
slightly arched, like the rings of a striped planet, but her
eyes narrowed in thought. She considered me; I balanced
against the light touch of her hand. At last she asked,
"Why were you sent to kill me?"

I told her, "I don't know."

I didn't know. I didn't *know*. The statement reverberated
through my head, the next few days, while I practiced my
sword-forms and was measured for new clothes, and tried
to figure out who I had become.

With the old Head of Ibex Company, I would have known.
Not directly—I wasn't a diplomat or a financial analyst—but
because I had been trained to infer his wishes. I could stand
behind his right shoulder, at a meeting with representatives
of another Company or merchants from a planet system,
and mark who was full of bravado, who needed a show of
force, who might strike to kill. But the old Head had retired
on the Ibex ship along with his favorite wife. He was writing
memoirs, now, or designing a better horse-embryo, or
whatever retired Heads did with their newfound time.

The new Head—my new boss—was young. Perhaps
four years younger than me. We had just missed each
other, at the Academy. He was clean-shaven, and affected
an enthusiasm for algorithmic planning, and I had done
my level best not to admit I didn't trust him.

I knew that the new Head was angry about something,
and that it involved the hundredships. But everything we
did involved the hundredships; it was who we were. We
traveled with the fleet, between star and star.

We traded information, gene designs, the finest scrolls, the lightest tapestries. But the bulk of my life—the bulk of all our lives—was spent in transit, wrapped inside a ship. The engine's blood, half supercooled and half alive, maintained the ship's sense of itself. We were *coherent*, cradled against the unreality that was the Deep.

I was a professional, a useful blade. Thus, when the Head first proposed transferring his base of operations to the khanym's hundredship, I memorized layouts and personnel. I learned a literal hundred engineers and pilots, and all the khanym's guards. When the Head chose a date to move, I crammed into the narrow ferryship with my single bag of gear. When he chose someone taller and more conventionally broad-shouldered to stand behind him in meetings with the khanym, I did not protest.

When he sent me to kill the khanym—I didn't protest then, either. With the old Head, I might have proffered a diplomatic suggestion. In the work of an assassin, eleven parts out of every dozen are understanding when not to kill. But I was so desperate to be recognized, to have my work measured and found worthy, that I clutched at the mission the moment it was offered.

Two of my counterparts' lives were wasted, and still I failed.

I did not spend all my own newfound time at the core of the hundredship. I visited gardens, and jogged along corridors, and drank sap-sweetened tea in tulip-shaped glasses. But everywhere I went I was marked, my head naked without a Company scarf, my hair too short for even the soldier's braid. This wasn't my home ship, so I knew few people outside Ibex Company. I had no desire to debrief with the Head's staff, and I certainly wasn't going to call Beylik.

It was easier to lounge at the khanym's feet, while she ran economic projections. I paid very little attention to the projections, though even I noticed they went up and then down. I thought a lot about doors, and monitors, and where a guard should stand. (Sometimes, naturally, I was one of those guards. When lounging, I was only half on duty.) I thought more about the khanym: the way her hair fell over her left shoulder, the way she always asked for fruit with tea. When she was thinking very hard, she would pause as if to bite her lower lip, and then make a tiny puffing noise instead. Sometimes her projections used color instead of lines. Then they glowed orange, like her favorite coat.

I recognized what was happening to me. I had been warned against it, when I studied to be a Company blade: sometimes, when you are protecting someone, the ideas of care get muddled in your mind, and you think they matter in ways that they do not. With the old Head, I had been safeguarded by his age; with the new Head, by his personality. I had no defense from the khanym. Her edged knives were inside my blood.

There was no use in speaking, and no possible reward. My over-honed attention would dull and change, the way all good things changed. I just had to wait.

I was telling myself so late one evening, for the ten millionth time, when the khanym said, "I have been arguing that we should sell the hundredships."

I straightened and asked, "Is this a test?"

The khanym's eyes crinkled in acknowledgment. She struck a couple of keys, and a schematic appeared on the large screen she kept to impress visitors. It showed a tracery of silver, its general form a teardrop, but with quills curved like ribs around a heart. I thought it was a drug at first, a framework for some protein. Then the view rotated and I read the scale.

"A satellite?"

"It's a ship, Tashnur. A ship without blood."

"How do you make a ship without blood?"

"You spin bone out of the weak places between the Deep and normal space."

I made a noise somewhere between confusion and disbelief, and she began telling me about energy differentials. Potential imbued the interface between space and the Deep. New techniques could channel that energy into a swiftly hardening matrix, without breaking its entanglements with itself. The khanym was no engineer: her skill was to hear what others said to her, to find the inner core of their intentions, and to channel that knowledge through her own conviction.

I admired the khanym's dedication to understanding. It was like my own practice with the sword, and yet unlike. But the conversation was already too abstract for me, so I offered a simpler observation: "This boneship is so little." It was an odd size, perhaps half the length of a hundredship: too small to hold a Company, too big to make a ferry.

"It's fast. The boneships can sink further, without being crushed."

The further you went into the Deep, the more you left behind the ordinary rules, effect and cause, the shape of light. We were scudding just under the surface, here, in our bubble of seeming reality. A ship that fell deeper could skip the usual comparisons of distance. "How much faster?"

"Twice as fast, now. In eighty years, as the planet-dwellers measure? Perhaps ten times."

Eighty years on a planet might mean twenty years for us: time crumpled, when you were slipping between stars. That was enough time for a child to grow to adulthood. It was enough time for our entire business to collapse. I understood the red and amber now, in the khanym's models.

"You think that we should buy a boneship?" I spoke to confirm that I had listened. But this was why the khanish office existed in the first place: someone had to make the long-term, strange decisions that involved all the ships and all the Companies. I didn't need to approve the reasoning. My job was to make sure the khanym survived long enough to enforce her decisions.

"I think that we should build them, for ourselves."

It would mean pausing, at some star. Being stuck in someone else's gravity, someone else's time. A change in all the Companies, every person trained again for some new skill. But the alternative was a cautious, slow collapse. I nodded, showing the weight of understanding.

We were silent for a while, the bone tracery revolving on the screen. At last the khanym said, "It is almost tomorrow. I suppose I will retire."

She reached out to help me rise, as if we were two friends sharing sesame cakes. Our hands were nearly the same size, though my nails were cut as short as I could manage, and hers were treated with a shimmering gloss. She tipped her head up very slightly, strands of her shining hair sliding across her shoulders and falling down her back. I realized I had held her hand too long, and that she knew it.

I stepped back, reciting an old lesson: "Khanym, I regret my impropriety. Please, let it mean nothing."

Her smiles were slightly too wide for her face, even the bitter ones. "Tell me, whom is it appropriate for a khanym to love?"

A person of no Company, and no other allegiances. A scholar, perhaps, if they cared for no secular advantage. A planet-dweller, if they would leave their planet. In other words, an impossible person.

I did not flee my enemies, but I fled the khanym's question, as decorously as I could manage.

Beylik messaged the next day, to ask if I would meet him. No conversation could be more uncomfortable than the one I had just survived, so I agreed. We walked in one of the hundredship's gardens, between trellises covered in pea vines. The lattices stretched from floor to ceiling. On the coreward side of each narrow passageway, the vines had pale pink flowers; on the hullward side, pods dangled, plump with lines of fruit.

Beylik and I traded bits of news about mutual acquaintances, the way you do when meeting somebody you once held close. He kept track of more people than I did. We had walked all the way to the garden's hullward edge before he said, "Tashnur, you don't have to do this."

"I think I do."

"I know it hurts, Tashnur. You've always been the very best. But—you're alive. You're still one of the best. You could come back to Ibex Company." The full-spectrum lights left dappled shadows on Beylik's turban. I had known all his braids and obligations, once, but now they were hidden from me.

"Did the Head tell you to talk to me?"

He stared at one of the laden pea-pods as if it held a rolled-up message, but at last said, "No."

Beylik tensed at even mild prevarication; he wouldn't tell an outright lie. Perhaps the Head had asked him to report contacts with me, after the fact.

I couldn't tell Beylik about the ships of bone, so I shoved my hands in the outer pockets of my new brown coat and explained the crystal shards floating in my blood. There was an old oath, when you swore to guard someone, or to love them: *I will stand behind you, as close as your own kidneys.* I made a joke of it, referencing the khanym's tiny knives. It was safer than telling him about the way the khanym stayed up late, turning her graphs and projections to find the whole fleet's benefit. It was definitely safer than explaining that she pushed her hair out of her face with both hands when she found a better way to present some information, or that her favorite slippers were striped with golden thread.

Beylik listened and was horrified, then quiet. I felt twisted up, guilty for confronting him with imagined pain. He was a tender person: a friend, but not the sort of friend who should see all of me. We walked back to the coreward edge of the pea trellises. Finally I asked, "Why did you message me?"

I expected a fumbling evasion, but Beylik shrugged and smiled. "Tashnur, I don't want to fuss, it's so small beside the changes in your life. But—I've been approved to raise a child. I'm transferring back to the Ibex hundredship on the next ferry."

I forced my own smile. "That is an honor. I'm so pleased for you." Only three of our old friends had been approved for children; we had just worked through the list, in catching up.

"Thank you." He shared with me a wealth of logistical detail: the ratings of the nursery co-op he had attended as a toddler, the latest research on synthesizing milk, the farewells he would make in the ten days before the ferryship left. We made the round of the trellises again.

We were nearly about to leave when Beylik said, "It's a shame, really, to leave work now. I had identified the most interesting star system."

"Interesting how?" I asked, already worried.

"Oh, there's not much in the way of people to trade with. One station, a handful of scientists monitoring a terraforming project. But the currents of the Deep run close to the surface there, and it's had some fascinating effects on planetary formation. There are two separate carbon planets of about the same mass as the silicate one, and in very tight orbits."

A carbon planet would mean deserts made of diamonds. Beylik had always had a taste for the romantic. But human access mattered more, here. "This shallow place—is it close to the terraformed planet?"

"Very. If you don't mind in-system drives."

It was the kind of place the khanym wanted, a system where we could settle, a system where we could grow ships. But that was a course the new Head of Ibex Company did not wish to take. No wonder he was packing my friend onto the ferryship.

I looked up at Beylik, my fear turning to sternness. "For the sake of the green ribbon that once bound us: if the

Head asks about our conversation, do not mention that you told me of this system."

"I don't see why it matters." He looked like I had given him the wrong mark on an exam.

"Do you promise?"

"I promise." Beylik ran his thumb along the edge of his beard. I could tell he wanted to trace the green cord he still wore.

In turn, I traced a vein down my neck to my collarbone. Then I turned the conversation back to smaller things, the mementoes he would pack, messages for friends on the Ibex hundredship. We walked out of the garden together, leaving behind the dappled light.

I wanted Beylik to focus on the khanym's knives. He didn't see the danger that the Head posed to him. But the danger would be there, the flip side of that so-convenient reproduction permit, as long as the Head believed that the link between us held. I needed to clarify my position.

My opportunity arrived the next day, when the khanym met with the Head of Ibex Company. They had agreed on a neutral conference room, its carpet shades of blue, its cushions moonlight-pale. I stood behind the khanym, to her right. I recognized the guard at the Head's shoulder. His name was Eshtanek; he tended to think too long when sparring, but used his reach to compensate. We watched each other while the khanym and the Head drank yogurt with mint—we called it yogurt, though on the hundredships it was mostly made of beans—and discussed the merits of a long-dead poet. It was not our turn to speak.

When the third cup was poured, the usual signal that business was at hand, the Head raised his eyes to me. "Tashnur. You would be welcome, on this side of the table."

"I cannot." I bowed, stiff-necked, the shallow side of rudeness. Eshtanek was glaring; I did not think he had anticipated this development.

"The crystal dart?" The Head's voice was gentle, in a way that might have been appropriate if he had been twice my age. "Tashnur, the khanym lied to you. There is no such technology."

I read, in the sudden perfection of the khanym's posture, the fact that he was right. My sword-hilt was on the sash at my waist; I grasped it, not trying to be subtle.

The Head smiled. "Tashnur. Welcome home."

He wanted me to kill her. He was offering me the option to undo my failure, to begin again. To serve a thriving Company for twenty years; and to be part of the long slide toward bankruptcy, after.

The khanym's hair, never braided, fell straight down her back and puddled behind her on the moonlight cushion. Not a strand of it moved.

I said, "I am already home." I put scorn into it, all the arrogance of an Academy senior; I wanted the Head to feel his relative youth. But I wanted the khanym to believe me, too.

She took a sip from her third cup.

Eshtanek's smile was mocking. The Head's seemed genuine; he was very good at selling things. "Of course." He took a document case from the floor beside him and laid it on the table, snapping the latches open.

I thought I hadn't pushed him hard enough. I needed him to hate me, instead of maneuvering to wield me.

The Head continued, "I think that you will find this proposal interesting."

I saw Eshtanek's horror first, and then the pistol. The Head gripped it two-handed, aiming at me, and released the safety. He had not lost his temper: it had evaporated in the bitter vacuum of his arrogance.

I could have thrown myself across the khanym. Knocked her down. Tried to soak up the momentum of a bullet, before it cut through her skin or through the skin of her ship.

I activated my blade.

In the fraction of a second where the Head could still believe I might obey, I extended my arm and lunged. My blade went through his throat. The pistol's muzzle rotated hullwards as it fell. It did not go off.

When your enemy is across the table, a pistol is a stupid weapon.

I said, "Eshtanek, I think that you should leave." He had a stunned look that I recognized; he did as he was told.

That left me alone with the khanym. She flipped the pistol's safety back again and replaced it in its case, careful to keep its point away from anyone alive. Because I am not a psychopath, I retracted my own blade and checked the pistol, removing the magazine and making sure the barrel was empty. I put it back in its case once more and offered the khanym my hand. She was very close to me, when she stood.

"I held you with a lie." The khanym's voice was soft, but not apologetic. Her lashes were thick, but a shade lighter than her hair, almost the color of my coat.

"The strength of a braid is not in its first crossing." I cupped my left hand against the khanym's cheek. It was a stupid thing to do, reckless, out of order. But my blood hummed with the knowledge that we were still alive, and I had left myself no other place to stand.

Her kiss tasted like mint and sharpness and the beginning of a star.

THE FIFTEENTH SAINT

in the year 3288 of the Nakhorian reckoning

SANNALI EMENEV DID two things with his life: he read a book with one page, and he ran a city.

Neither of these was his official role. There were eight judges in Junpalto. Every one of the eight of them got up in the morning, pulled a stretchy cap over their braided hair, placed a flowing wig over the cap, and sat in state to hear the problems of the city. But the first judge was brand new, the second was exhausted, the third was busy looking after his aging father, and the fourth was distracted by bickering among the Companies. So it ran through the list, and the conclusion was that if you needed someone to rearrange a department or reform a school, you spoke to Judge Emenev.

The book was private. Emenev rarely spoke of it, even
to his clerk: it was the sort of thing hermits in the canyons
or starfarers who had listened to voices in the deep cared
about, not rational and responsible city folk. But Emenev
had seen too many lives twist from oath to debt to quiet
desperation to sneer at luck, whatever form it came in.
So every morning, after he pulled the soft cap over his
head but before he took his wig from its stand, Emenev
removed the book's silk wrapper, spun the old-fashioned
multi-dial lock till it revealed the initials of the prophets,
opened the cover, and said, "Good morning."

The book responded with a line of praise for the sun
that was or the sun that is or the stars scattered through
the deep. From there, it jumped directly to advice. The
book held the wisdom of fourteen saints. In the chilled
silicon and indium alloys pressed between its enamel
covers there was a further, coordinating wisdom, to
predict the fable each reader would need before they
thought to require it. Interpreting the results was a
different problem. Emenev kept a hand-written notebook
on real paper with questions in the top half of each page.
Sometimes he even went back and filled in a column of
answers.

On that particular early autumn morning, Emenev
had lain in bed longer than usual, pondering a question
of contracts and watching the shadows on his ceiling
turn from patches of lighter and darker gray to squares
to sharp-edged latticework. He finally tore himself out of
bed when he heard, or hoped he heard, a sound below.
Thus, his greeting to the book was perfunctory. The book
responded with two lines of verse:

THE PLANET TIDE DRAWS THE MOUNTAINS
HIGHER THAN THE SKY.
BELOVED, IS THAT MOON-DUST,
OR A WAVE BREAKING?

Emenev preferred the adventures of saints and livestock to the book's more poetic excursions. He scribbled "mountains— dust—wave" in his notebook, then hastened down broad steps to the breakfast room.

The courtyard doors were closed, but the glass had turned transparent, letting light pour in. Emenev poured tea from the urn on the sideboard into a flared cup, rolling the word "beloved" round his mouth, then pushing it back with "moon-dust". When he turned back toward the windows, a man was waiting.

The man, whom Emenev knew as Kiza, had a compact build, and that morning he was clean-shaven, which made him seem younger than his thirty-odd years. His smile for Emenev was merry. But Emenev stood still for a moment, caught not so much by Kiza's expression as by the light. It shone through Kiza's unbound hair like the banked glow of polished garnet.

That free fall of waist-length hair meant possibility. Kiza was what people called a tongue for hire. He could be anyone or no-one, a soldier or failed poet or Company man, as each mission required. Emenev, whose hair beneath his cap was twisted up with ribbon for his brother's daughter and his youngest sister's child and four distinct professional societies, shivered at the flaunted freedom. Instead of reaching out, he bowed and asked, "Will you have tea?"

Kiza laughed at him and gripped his shoulder. "Sani, I can find my own tea in your house."

Kiza's fingers were strong. Emenev, who moved with the habitual care of someone who had grown too tall too fast, longed to fling his arms wide and crush the man against him. But there was an order to even this most unheralded of duties. Emenev filled a tray with luxurious and unlaborious foods: cubes of melon fresh from the mountains, pâté of duck marbled with berries, crackers with sesame and black cumin. Kiza did pour his own tea, taking the opportunity to add an extra spoonful of jam.

They demolished the stacks of food together, brushing fingers against fingers in competition for the ripest chunks of fruit. Emenev tried to talk about velo-polo like an ordinary person. Kiza, who knew perfectly well how to play, asked sillier and sillier questions: There were always four riders to a team? Never five, or a threesome? These mallets, they were of a standard size? Did the judge not prefer an extra-long polo stick?

But when at last Emenev toppled into helpless laughter, Kiza said sternly, "Sani. Tell me what you need," and despite Emenev's many desires, they were instantly in the realm of business.

"I need you to go to Tengiz-Ushiyet."

"Ah, a holiday by the sea. With the entire Western Army." Kiza spun his hair out of his face in a temporary twist, leaving his stern gaze unimpeded. "Why now? Why not ten days ago?"

Ten days ago, the army had moved into Ushiyet. The news bulletins made cheerful noises about the importance of practicing urban maneuvers and extra discounts on military wheat. It wasn't unusual for a group of officers to grow bored and decide they wanted more parades and less supervisory farming. A brief incursion wasn't cause for alarm.

But Emenev could not be calm. He offered his first uneasy piece of evidence: "The judges there aren't talking. Last week, I sent their second judge white tea. She hasn't answered." You didn't hold a meeting without food or drink, not even a virtual one; you didn't accept tea without a meeting. The etiquette breach rang like a siren.

Once Emenev had started noticing the strangeness, other facts piled up. Half of the news bulletins were recycled from another year, though the scenes of cheering crowds seemed current. The price of emmer was rising. The Pellona Company had moved its base of operations to the southeast.

"All the nodes in the Ushiyet lattice are stuffed with bonfire footage," Kiza told him.

"You watch that stuff?"

"You don't?"

"It's animated rumor. Stories without roots."

Kiza stilled his hands. "There's a brand new story about setting bus tires on fire, Sani. What were you going to do? Wait for the warranty complaint?"

"I was going to send you!" Emenev spoke in haste, and then repeated, with more care, "I am sending you."

Emenev was not a stranger to arranging people's lives. But usually the key term was arrangement. He took scores on the proficiency exams or arrays of past performance metrics and combined them, bringing people together or apart the way his windows brightened or darkened against the flow of sunlight. He was sending Kiza to a city overrun by soldiers. There was no projection he could run, to evaluate this choice. Emenev saw moss-gray uniforms in his mind's eye, rows of rifles. He watched the loose shirt fall away from Kiza's wrists, and thought of those hands holding a pistol steady. Emenev was responsible. If Kiza died, or if Kiza shot someone—a situation could change that quickly, a wall of glass crumbling into razor-sparkling dust.

"Keep an eye on the nodes, Sani. I'll go fishing on the pier." Kiza pressed a charm into Emenev's hand: a cheap thing, mass-produced for a mass-venerated saint, a bead and tassel stamped with curving thorns. It felt too light; Emenev had to focus, not to drop it. When he pried the bead apart, there would be a code inside.

Meanwhile, Kiza had produced a long, light scarf. He held one end in his mouth as he wrapped the turban round his head, rapidly and neatly. You would never know his hair was unbraided, underneath. He shrugged into a jacket sewn with many pockets, ducked his head, and seemed, for a moment, ordinary and unremarkable.

"Be careful," Emenev told him. That was easier than asking, "Is the wave about to break?"

Kiza left, laughing.

AT THE END of the week, Emenev took the bus to visit his mother. There was a stop a block from the judicial chambers, and no transfers. The bus chose its routes based on demand; Emenev wondered whether he had made this trip often enough to shift the route all by himself.

Emenev's mother still lived in the same two-room flat that he had grown up in. He had offered to find her a house: diffidently, when he was first enrolled as an advocate, then more strenuously, when he became a judge and she began to complain that her knees crackled on the stairs. But she insisted that she was too old to change her ways, that the noodle-shop on the corner and the grocer round the block would be lost without her patronage, and no number of forceful representations would shift her. Instead, the family clustered around her. There were no longer five of them packed into the apartment—it had been six, while the contract for his youngest sister's parentage lasted—but Emenev's brother took the flat above, and his middle sister found a flat next door. The youngest sister had made it all the way to a block with a different noodle-shop and a different bus line. Emenev was the only one who had left the neighborhood, and the only one without children. He bought ice cream and raspberry-whiteplum sauce at the grocer as a distraction.

Emenev needn't have worried. He opened the door and walked straight into an argument. His niece was

shouting and his brother was holding a glass of vodka
and pontificating right in the middle of the arch between
Emenev and the kitchenette. He waded gingerly through
the fray, managing not to swing the bags into a lamp
or a child, glared his brother out of the archway, kissed
his mother, and embarked on making space in the cold
storage with the dedication of a man who could have been
an architect.

The fight raged on. Emenev's sister-in-law offered to
find spoons for the fruit sauce. In the main room, his niece
shouted, "The grader isn't even alive!"

Emenev and his sister-in-law despaired of finding metal
spoons that matched, and settled on the compostable
sorghum kind. As she passed him the box, his sister-in-law
told him quietly, "Simet failed the literature practical."

"But she's a good writer."

Emenev had misjudged the ambient roar, or else grown
too used to projecting through a courtroom, because his
niece spun toward the kitchenette, child's braid swinging.
"I am an incredible writer! That's the problem. I had an
original idea!"

Emenev sighed, grabbed a piece of flatbread with extra
onions, and committed himself to the investigation.

Simet had taken a classic poem of two centuries past,
where an incarnation of the Divine was seen feeding
pigeons in a park, and reinterpreted it as political allegory.
As the Divine flickered between old and young and
middle-aged, between wrinkled cheeks and springing
black beard, she (and he, and they) represented three
enduring power groups: the judges, the army, and the
Companies. "The judge is the old woman, Uncle Nalek,
because she remembers everything."

"Thank you," Emenev said, dryly. "Who are the
ordinary people, in your analysis?"

"That's the best part. They're the student who watches the
transformation. Because a student can become anything!"

Simet actually believed it. She thought that if she studied hard and chose the right advanced exams, she could win an officer's commission or a Company apprenticeship or become a judge. The proof of the third option's validity stood beside her, balancing a piece of flatbread on a napkin.

But Emenev had never trusted that preparedness would be enough. It must be a marvelous thing, he mused, to reach adolescence with two parents in a permanent contract and a bedroom to yourself. You could reduce an entire incarnation to a metaphor, rather than begging the Divine for luck. He asked, "What was your counterthesis?"

"I didn't have one."

"Every essay has a counterthesis," Emenev's brother intoned, surely not for the first time.

"Not in the same essay! If I was an advocate in Uncle Nalek's courtroom, someone else would give the counterthesis and then he would synthesize. I kept writing my thesis because it was *good*!"

"The grader didn't think so," snapped her father.

"The grader is a machine."

"It's a machine intelligence, guided by the practice of an expert teacher," Emenev interposed. "It has to be that way, for consistent grading. Every fourteen-year-old on this continent takes the literature exam."

"Every fourteen-year-old everywhere has been taking a literature exam since before I was born. For all I know, the teacher is dead. They're a ghost. I was marked unsatisfactory by a ghost."

A "Fair" mark was a graceful failure. This was worse: one unsatisfactory exam could wreck a lyceum admission. "In some cases, exams can be retaken," Emenev suggested.

"But it's not my fault! It's the ghost's fault, for not seeing a good essay."

"How would the new exam be arranged?" Simet's father asked.

Emenev's instinct was to fold his hands and project thoughtfulness, but the flatbread was in the way. "The most usual justification is illness. I don't know all the contingencies. I might chat with the head of the lyceum."

"What about the others?" Simet demanded. She swayed with the intensity of her emphasis like a birch tree by the river. She had the family height.

"What others?"

"Every fourteen-year-old on this continent takes the exam, Uncle Nalek." Simet matched his intonation precisely. "How many failed because the ghost hates a good thesis?"

"Machine intelligences are not supernatural." Emenev was letting her set the terms of the discussion. The whole situation felt like a tea glass about to slide over the edge of the tray.

He should not have been glad when the comm folded into the brim of his hat started buzzing. Only a few people could force the physical alert.

Emenev took the phone call on the balcony, wedging himself between a swaddled umbrella and a planter full of bedraggled stewfruit vines. The caller was his clerk, Notary-General Umirvayet. Her voice was rougher than usual, her apologies perfunctory.

"What has the fourth judge done?" Emenev asked.

"Judge Rustamov is calling on the second judge for a curfew. You've seen the news?"

"A Fourthday evening curfew? What resin have they smoked?" Half of the city would be visiting family; the rest were in the tea-shops, or resting up for Fifthday.

"We need visuals, Judge."

Emenev pulled his tablet from his pocket and unfolded it, balancing the screen on the balcony railing. He felt like a teenager sneaking outside to read radical newspapers.

Umirvayet was still in her office. The light cast cold blue shadows, hollowing her cheeks and sharpening her chin. She flicked her fingers, and the view changed to a railway station somewhere in the mountains: ticket kiosks with conical roofs, an empty platform, the rails, a stretch of gravel filmed with early snow, and then the cliffs beyond. "It's Yashmu Pass," Umirvayet told him.

The film had the silver border and second-by-second timestamp of judicial footage. Emenev watched the platform, waiting for a suspect, trying to ignore the black bird pecking at something on the tracks. He overlooked the first slipping in the cliff face, the shift that could have been the camera swerving, if it hadn't been set into the station roof. A few moments later the entire cliff was moving, sliding down like overheated butter. Dust and smoke foamed up. The camera did shake now, along with the building holding it.

The view resolved to a mess of boulders and flashing lights—amber, red, and one insistent white pulse at the peak of the remaining kiosk that Emenev recognized as *Approaching train*. "Luck?" he asked.

"The Gentian freight was running three minutes late."

The footage couldn't show the frantic whistle of a train trying to slow. At least gravity was on its side. Emenev realized he was breathing in time with the flashing light, and forced his chest out, then in. The snub-nosed engine pushed into sight at last, coasting, coasting, but with thousands of tons behind it. There was a big round eye painted on its side, the hallmark of an expert system, with a gentian flower in the center.

The train finally paused, perhaps a meter from the closest scattered boulder. Emenev imagined its eye closing in relief. But a figure in mud-and-pine camouflage was approaching. Here the footage ended.

The figure had been wearing a uniform designed for the side of the mountains where rain fell steadily, so Emenev's first question was, "Has the Western Army made a statement?"

"They recommend civilians and Company employees avoid Yashmu Pass for the next two weeks, due to ongoing operations."

It was a plain statement of a huge fact. Society was an awning supported by four poles: the law-courts, the armies, the Companies, and the people. But the Western Army was challenging the Companies and the cities simultaneously. A collapsing tent; dust like sea-foam; mountains breaking like waves. Emenev ran his thumb along the edge of his tablet, as if he could draw up a message from Kiza. Inside the flat, his brother was declaiming.

Umirvayet was silent. "Go home," Emenev told her. "Before the second judge approves this curfew. I'll call her next."

The call ended. Emenev let the screen of his tablet darken and stood for a moment, watching the reflected lights: white dots from the apartment across the way, where they knew nothing, and golden oblongs from his mother's lamps. He should warn his mother he would need a bed, before he called the judge. He folded his screen and dove into the noise.

THE EIGHT JUDGES of Junpalto met the next morning. They sat at an octagonal table in their accustomed places, their wigs freshly combed, with their clerks behind them to provide necessary documents, and sipped espresso from tiny cups. There should have been breakfast, but none of the kitchen staff worked on Fifthday. Emenev had acquired a box of fried pastries on the way from his mother's flat to the meeting.

The sixth judge took a small one, which showered her napkin with powdered sugar. At least the wigs were already white.

They began by discussing the city's reaction to the news. Grumbling; fear; as yet no outright panic. The second judge, Nurlanevet, suggested an extension of the curfew as a precautionary measure. The sixth judge set aside her pastry and concurred.

"Out of an excess of caution," Judge Rustamov proposed, "shall we shift the curfew's beginning up to seven?"

"It's still light outside at that hour," Emenev protested.

"All the more reason to discourage gatherings." Rustamov, the fourth judge, was classically handsome: brow high like an icy moon, lips full beneath a neatly curled mustache. He pressed his fingers together as if posing for his municipal portrait.

Emenev set his espresso cup down with a click. "What does my esteemed colleague imagine people will eat?"

"Healthful food, that they prepare themselves, in the kitchens of their homes?"

Emenev could not jump down the fourth judge's throat. He wiped his mouth with his napkin instead, envying his colleague's deftness, his economy of motion. "The average citizen of Junpalto has eight square meters of living space. They have no room for a pantry and cold storage. They barely have room for a double bed."

"I delight in my colleague's command of demographic statistics."

Emenev nodded, projecting false collegial amusement. In truth, he knew the number because he had reveled in exceeding it, when as a newly minted advocate he rented an apartment by himself.

"But surely," Rustamov continued, "our citizens can purchase bread and salad, as they wend home from work? Assembly of a meal is not beyond their skills?"

Emenev had been to formal dinners at the fourth judge's house. They all had. The man had a live-in cook.

"I believe Seventh Judge Emenev is concerned for the grocers?" the sixth judge interposed. "We cannot ask them to live in their places of business! We will also wish to make provisions for restaurateurs, and to consider the impact on tourism more broadly."

They were back in the realm of reasonable plans and contingencies: rules to make, policies to apply, and strategies to redirect supply chains, now that freight from the western coast was unavailable. It was a frustrating task for a Fifthday morning, and Emenev could have used some of his book's wisdom, but they managed it.

They managed with all the more vigor because they were avoiding a bigger question, one Judge Nurlanevet finally raised several hours into the meeting, after they had broken for tea and an odd collection of crisps: "How will we respond when the Western Army arrives on our doorstep?"

In this group, Emenev was the brash one, the one who spoke difficult truths out loud, so he squared his shoulders and said, "We must summon the Lake Army first."

Rustamov smiled. Perhaps he thought summoning an army was like hiring an expert in unclogging drains. The eighth judge laughed in shock, then tried to squash it, shaking their head till their long earrings vibrated like springs.

Nurlanevet was square and sure. All of her leisure activities had solidity: splitting wood for the fire at lakefront cottages, or crafting earthenware vases. She looked now as if she had been awake all night, guarding some small and precious creature through a desperate illness. "Will the Lake Army protect our citizens? Will they seek justice?"

"Second Judge, I apologize for making a statement of consummate baldness," said the third judge, who never did anything of the sort. "But I must attempt a response to your cogent question. It seems, from my perspective, after considering the multitude of factors, that it is imperative we contemplate whether, in the alternative, we are prepared, ourselves, to fight a war."

"We don't know how," said Emenev.

All of the other judges had to have their say, but that, in the end, was that.

The afternoon was consumed by crafting the text of the invitation and adorning it with flourishes. Emenev signed with his gaudiest stylus, the one whose cap was starred with artificial diamond. Umirvayet contacted the florist outside the Lake Army base and ordered a massive arrangement, full of sword lilies and tulips opening like suns. The first judge's clerk, who was as experienced as that judge was new, set up a meeting with a general.

They channeled the general's image into a globe at the center of the table. She stood in a well-lit room, the sword lilies behind her. Her uniform was the color of dried grass. Her graying hair was pulled back from her face and braided with ribbons of sky blue, for officers swore a single oath and a single devotion, and hers was to the army of the lakes.

The judges read their invitation, the clauses rolling off their tongues. Even the third judge's voice was firm and sonorous. It fell to Emenev to ask, "Will you, having considered all these factors, come to the aid of the city of Junpalto?"

It took skill for the general to look him in the eye, with a full globe of spaces stretched across her screen, but she managed it. She smiled the smile one makes at a cat boldly capturing a beetle, and answered, "We will come."

THE SUN WAS sinking behind the Company financiers' towers by the time Emenev approached his house.

He was the only person on his street; lights brightened and darkened at the top of the compound walls, tracing his movements. He passed through his wooden gates with their linked octagonal carvings, changed his sharp-toed shoes for slippers, and was at last in his own home. He stretched, feeling the welcoming emptiness: no extra chairs to trip on, no nicked tables swathed in machine-embroidered tablecloths, and for that matter no subordinates juggling styluses or shelves filled with unread legal tomes. He patted his couch like an old friend, drawing his fingertips along the linen grain, then went upstairs to find the book.

The book gave him a fable about a widow, a goat, a mountain lion, a box of eggs packed in tissue, and a river crossing. The moral was that the ferryman was the only one to profit.

"Friend," Emenev told it, "I am doing my best."

The columns of text shivered like rain, then re-formed. The new text began with a litany: an electron's internal spin, the electron dancing around a nucleus, the shiver of atoms within a rock, all the way up to the slow rotation of the galaxy's arms and the slide of entire galaxies. Twisted behind and within and around all of these things was the deep, that other space where starships cut between stars. At every shift in scale, the book said, we experience a loss. But at every shift in scale there is the deep; thus at every shift in scale we find eternity; at every shift in scale there is the beloved, who has always been beloved.

Emenev felt both too large and too small. He shook himself all over, thanked the book, and allowed himself to open his everyday tablet and run through the sequence that would check for messages from Kiza, on some anonymous node. A message was there, wrapped tight, with the sparkling and obvious encryption used for letters to lovers. Emenev fed in the code from Kiza's bead.

The recording opened on Kiza, balancing on a railing by the harbor. He had found a tourist's windbreaker somewhere, the kind with too many zippers. Sunlight made the fabric into mirrors and shadows, like the water behind him. "You won't believe it here!" he told the hovering camera, his smile as sharp as fresh-cut sheets of paper.

Kiza cupped the camera in both hands and drew it toward him; it buzzed against his fingers like a fortunate bee. "It's not just the army. It's the army and the citizens together. They've found philosophy. Humans as shepherds. Every one of us, the Divine Guide in miniature. No machine intelligence without human direction."

Kiza released the camera and it spun upwards in a lazy spiral. "No more saints! Nothing between us and the Divine!" Behind him there were yachts, pedal-boats, and a stacked three-level water-bus. It had eyes on its prow for the navigation system, but someone had sprayed them with a shining X, too bright for blood.

"I think you should stop working. I'm serious. Go on a long vacation." Just a flicker, there, of the bone-deep emptiness of a city lost. Then Kiza laughed and told the camera, "When I see you again, I'm going to hug you so hard, you'll think the ocean hit you."

The message broke into soap-bubble fragments. Emenev was too wise to have saved it anyway; or so he told himself.

He did not consider heeding his friend's warning. He did not know where he could go, beyond Junpalto. Emenev swallowed his worry like a string of tourmaline beads, suppressing all the questions about Kiza's stylized lies, and occupied himself in crafting a reply. He drew a rotating model of a sky-blue ribbon, the Lake Army's color, woven and knotted with the translucent gold of his own personal contracts.

Kiza had been a Lake Army soldier, before he set allegiances aside. Twelve years and out. But Kiza did not make promises, so he had no ribbon color.

THE NEXT FEW weeks were too long, and their days were too short. The Companies cancelled conferences; the price of tea shot up anyway. The municipal soup kitchens doubled their capacity. Shops sold out of cured cheese and winter coats.

Emenev talked panicked administrators through rescheduling four major court cases, sponsored an emergency budget addendum for the kitchens, and organized an audit of the city's water supply. He made lists on his tablet and lists of lists by hand. He felt as crumbly as overstirred cement.

He rode the bus in the morning, and home again at night. He could have crushed himself into a velokab and been there faster. But there were wild hares living in the square near his house, chewing on the ornamental bushes, their patchy fur shading from gravel-flecked to white. The bus gave him scraps of time to notice these things, to wonder why this woman always carried an umbrella or that shop was painted in concentric squares, without having to create a policy or render a judgment.

He had more time to wonder because the buses were running more and more slowly, as if they too were overwhelmed by expectations. Sometimes they approached the square and then veered off. Waiting people traced the dots on their tablets and cursed. Emenev preferred to watch the hares.

A morning came when Emenev thought the bus would
not arrive at all. Other riders summoned velokabs,
cursing, or jogged toward distant trams. At last, only
Emenev and the woman with the umbrella remained. The
bus, when it finally appeared, seemed ordinary: a bright
oblong, its curving windows overlaid with advertisements
for healthy habits, like an overpriced vitamin pill. It
leaned toward the curb and opened the center hatch. The
woman moved forward, using the point of her umbrella
for balance, and collapsed into the nearest seat. Emenev
sat near her. There were clusters of teenagers in the front
and back of the bus, laughing and pointing at the time on
the overhead clock. A person in a pin-dotted turban was
having a vociferous argument with their tablet.

"Rerouting," the bus said, in a confident tenor.

The back-of-bus teenagers waved their arms, palms
turned toward the ground and thumbs outstretched in
the universal symbol for "Next stop!" The front-of-bus
teenagers cheered. The turbaned person made a noise like
a stalling helicopter.

"Bus, explain the route change," Emenev said, with
the forced calm that evaded pre-programmed requests for
patience.

"Rerouting to Broad Avenue to mitigate demand,"
the bus told him, its own patience inexhaustible. It took a
sharp left toward the city center, ignoring the teenagers'
pleas; their noises rose in pitch.

Emenev pulled his tablet out and checked the bus map.
The only purple dots he could find were on Broad Avenue,
crawling back and forth. "Bus, make immediate stop as
requested."

"Next stop Broad and Third," the bus announced.

That was a good half-hour away. Even the front-of-bus
teenagers were glancing at the bright-orange Emergency
Stop switch and murmuring. The penalty for non-
emergency use was dire.

Emenev was the seventh judge of Junpalto. He refused to be kidnapped by a bus. He rose to his feet, balancing easily against the bus's movement, and yanked the switch down.

"Emergency stop requested. All systems nominal. Seeking safe egress." Pulsing lights lit up around the bus as it swung toward the curb. All the hatches lifted; the teenagers spilled onto the street; the turbaned person stomped away.

"And you, khaniet?" Emenev asked the woman with the umbrella, offering her the old-fashioned honorific.

"I'm not walking home," she informed him, with all the decision of the ancient khans. Pain pulled the lines beneath her eyes at a diagonal.

"Khaniet, I would be delighted to summon a velokab on your behalf—"

"I don't want favors. I want my due. Barley porridge at the city kitchen, and a ride home on the city bus."

"But khaniet, you can see that there is a malfunction."

"Then fix it! Aren't you a city worker?" She gestured at his coat. Its wide trim and shining buttons echoed the city insignia.

"Resuming service," the bus announced. "Next stop, Broad and Third."

In booming courtroom voice, Emenev declaimed, "Bus, as seventh judge and representative of the city of Junpalto, I order you to proceed to the nearest municipal kitchen with dispatch."

"That's a fine attempt," the woman told him, "and your beard is thick enough. But judges don't ride the bus."

The title only went so far, without the wig and the bundle of official ribbons. Emenev wondered whether he should bleach extra silver in his beard.

The bus was moving again, trundling back into the road as if this was an ordinary day in an ordinary year. "Next stop, Broad and Third." Emenev felt the traffic as pressure on his chest, the weight of a river. He might flail and flail and never emerge.

But that would entail ceasing to work, and Emenev would not permit himself to cease. A technician should understand this route deviation. Emenev was not a technician, so he messaged his clerk, "Who holds the support contract for the city buses?"

Umirvayet answered, "Zato. They're a Fountain Company subsidiary, out of Tengiz-Ushiyet."

A dead end, then. Tengiz-Ushiyet might have created the problem; it would not solve it. Emenev pondered whom else he might know who would understand the mind of a machine and reached the obvious and unsettling conclusion. He contacted his house system and asked to speak to the book.

"I apologize for contacting you in this manner," he began. The book had preferences, and one of them was to behave like a book, not a shadow of a human architect.

"You would not disturb us without need," the book said briskly. "But state your business. Don't delay for earthly ceremony."

Emenev told his tale. After a whirring pause, like the flicker of thousands of pages, the book replied, "WHERE ARE THE SHIPS THAT ROAM THE DEEP NO LONGER? WHERE ARE THE STARS THAT FALL FROM THE LONG DANCE?"

Emenev thanked the book, ended the call, and pondered what it meant.

"I'm sorry, khaniet. This will be loud." He rose to his full height, bellowing for power, and slammed against the back of the seat before him. It didn't budge. Emenev was tall and strong, but compared to a late-night crowd of tourists he was a gently floating petal. He punched a window; he hurt nothing but his wrists.

"Please respect the comfort of other citizens," said the bus. "Next stop, Broad and Third!"

Kiza would have produced a pistol, or a knife, or a piece of metal that expanded to a lever. He would have a mental catalog of ways to break buses. Emenev had a tablet and a pen.

This was not entirely correct: Emenev had a tablet
and a stylus. The stylus cap shone with plasma-deposited
diamond. He scrubbed it against the glass. It left a white
line and a trail of grit. That would work, then. Steadying
himself, Emenev wrote a message above several seats,
in three well-spaced columns. The hatched and shaded
letters embraced in flourishes: "Sani loves Kiza." It was a
stupid message, a doomed adolescent promise—the classic
style, for some strategic vandalism.

"If it pleases you, will you complain, khaniet?" Emenev
asked. "I hope to find some answers at the station."

The woman rapped her umbrella's handle on the seat
and declared, "Bus! This window has been vandalized!"

Lights trailed across the ceiling as the bus's internal
cameras assessed the damage. A jet of water sprayed over
the window. Kiza's name gleamed.

"Leaving service for necessary repairs," the bus
announced at last. "Please exit at your earliest convenience.
This is the last scheduled stop." But Emenev remained, as
did the woman with the umbrella.

The ride to the bus depot was long, long enough for
Emenev to wonder what would happen if he simply
disappeared, swept out of place like a game-piece caught
on a sleeve. He could ask the same question, on a grander
scale, about his entire city: if the Lake Army never
arrived, if Junpalto was overrun, who would know? It
was one city, on one plain, on one less-than-populated
continent, on one world.

It was dangerous, these days, for thoughts to pause—
like a short rest in a midwinter snowdrift. Emenev set
himself, instead, to learn his companion's life story. She
had been an aide to an elderly scholar, until her joints
rebelled and she could no longer manage the necessary
lifting, even with mechanical assist; her pension had gone
to pay her first child's gambling debts. Her second child
led snowshoe treks from a mountain town so isolated it lost

lattice access when the snowpack grew. In return, Emenev gave the woman profiles of all his siblings' children.

"But you have none yourself?" she demanded, with the authority of the old.

Ordinarily Emenev pled the exigencies of running a city. This time he offered a different slice of truth: "I'd hoped for a long-term contract. Not a temporary marriage."

"That's a luxury for folks who come from money. Your Kiza doesn't need you to buy eternal love. Enjoy the days you have with him, as they come."

There were so many assumptions bundled into that remark—who Emenev's family was, what his relationships might be—that Emenev despaired of sorting them. He gave her the real answer as a joke: "Kiza is a glamorous corporate spy. I don't think he'll ever settle, even temporarily."

She sensed the edge in his reply, if not its source, and turned to looking out the windows, commenting on the long rows of warehouses that marked the transition from city into prairie. "There's a bus," she said, after a while.

There was a bus behind them, and another bus parked by the side of the road, the solar panels along its roof-spine gleaming in the sun. Then there were two buses at the edge of the road, then six. Then it became impossible to remark on a single bus. They lined the roadside in a single shimmering line, not quite still, but edging softly forward like accumulating snow.

The depot gate slid open, and the depot was before them. It was tiled with octagons and squares, like any municipal building, but these octagons were almost as tall as Emenev. Only the tacked-on side office was human scale. Emenev pulled the emergency stop lever one more time and escorted his companion inside. They found a single day attendant, a young man with wide-set eyes and fluffy beard.

The municipal system gave the attendant Emenev's name and titles, in a scrolling stripe at the left edge of his screen.

He found the woman a chair, failed to take her umbrella, offered tea, and panicked.

"Tea!" said Emenev. "Tea is ideal." The depot's cupboards were sadly lacking in amenities—it seemed that managerial meetings took place in the city—so he used his sundries account to liberate puffed chickpeas and a selection of wafers from the vending machine, and they sat down to an impromptu meeting.

After stumbling through the pleasantries, the attendant admitted he had expected a follow-up from the fourth judge's office, which monitored physical infrastructure, not a visit from the seventh judge. The woman with the umbrella was simply watching, brows angled together: if Emenev was a real judge, her manner implied, then anything was possible.

"What have you reported to Judge Rustamov?"

The attendant spoke in bursts of nouns: "night," "ice," "pallet." He had not personally reported anything, Emenev deduced: that was the night manager's duty. But the meteorological projection said winter storms would arrive early this year, and a shipment the depot needed had been delayed. "Won't go. Esteemed judge. The buses, they won't go."

"Can you show me?" Emenev asked.

He expected some report, perhaps a map. Instead, the attendant said, "Authorize equipment? Esteemed judge?" and tossed him a helmet, earmuffs, and a neon bracelet. "For safety."

"Is there a standard safety training?"

There was. Emenev listened to the full quarter-hour with attention, tightened the helmet straps under his chin, flipped the bracelet's "This is a human" marker to "present," and was at last ready to enter the machines' part of the building.

The light on that side was bright and flat, the ceiling high. Robots swarmed the bus, scooting back and forth on dozens of swiveling wheels. They seemed independent, almost alive, though that was an illusion: the true intelligence was built into the building, watching from the girders with linked camera-eyes.

"Tires," said the attendant. Emenev heard the word through his earmuffs, the human voice high and sharp against the background roar. He looked, obediently. A robot took each tire, balancing it on evenly spaced claws. The back tires slid away to the far end of the vast room. Two free-standing axes shot forward, and the robots mounted the front tires upon them. They proceeded to peel the tires, as one slips cherry skin from stewed and sugared fruit.

Robots peered over the inner toruses, prodding them and strengthening patches with bursts of sparks. Then they transferred them to a new station and drew out strips of tough and corrugated rubber, wrapping the tires as they turned. A sliding knife cut the new ridges even deeper. These were tires built for a Junpalto winter, meant to grip pavement in temperatures a West Continent manufacturer couldn't even imagine.

More robots wrapped the tires, clad in their new armour, in a rubbery bag, sucking the air from it. They transferred them to a vast tank and shut the door. A display began counting down from an hour; the facility was not above a bit of showmanship for human visitors.

"Where did the back tires go?" Emenev asked.

"Back tires recycled. Front tires to the back. New on the front. Esteemed judge."

"Where are the new tires?"

The attendant ducked his head as far as he could manage while wearing a helmet and earmuffs. "Tengiz-Ushiyet."

Emenev, who customarily strove not to invoke powers he could not know or placate, swore with false gentleness, "Eyes of the Divine." It was the most foolish, basic logistics problem, the kind of thing his niece learned in games at school. The depot system expected tires to be delivered, and humans expected the system to winter-proof the buses. With freight stuck at the pass, all the buses in the city were waiting, waiting, shifting back and forth in line for a refit that never came. "Can we remount the old tires, while we reroute from the south?"

"Fourth judge. Not authorized. Esteemed judge."

What good was a judgeship, if one could not arrange things? "If you will both excuse me, I will place a call."

Emenev went outside to speak to Umirvayet. She contacted the fourth judge's office, almond cookies and tea changed hands, and in only half an hour, Emenev was speaking to Rustamov directly.

"My dear colleague, where *are* you?" Rustamov began.

"At the municipal bus repair facility. I apologize for the noise." Buses were still creeping toward the building, shifting forward in their long, weird line.

"I know you enjoy the role of the ordinary townsman, but this is pure excess. Wasn't one bus enough?"

Emenev smiled wide and wished he had a cookie to bite into. "That's the problem, you see. All of the city buses are stuck here."

The fourth judge's mouth curved in gentle, forbearing amusement. It was the expression he would use to revoke a professional license, or to sentence a thief. "You called me out of a Pellona Company arbitration to play bus conductor?"

"City transit has come to a stop. The expert system can't handle the supply disruptions, with the pass closed."

"Emenev, my good friend. We are all working on the troubles caused by the pass closure. If the Companies start rerouting investments because they don't trust our authority, we will have more trouble than a few late shopkeepers."

"Forgive me, Rustamov. This need not be a major operation. I simply need an authorization from your office. A single seal."

"I see. These little difficulties are so irksome, are they not? My wife's child has been having all sorts of trouble with his lyceum entrance—I believe his physics scores aren't where they should be, which a ridiculous quibble, when he plans to study law—and if I try to say something, well, there's no harm in it, but one doesn't like to look particular. Of course your staff is in and out of the schools all the time."

Emenev could speak to the lyceum's head. He had said as much to Simet. But he heard her in his mind, declaring, "Every fourteen-year-old on this continent takes the exam," standing straight as a tree in springtime. What kind of a judge was he, if he didn't listen?

What kind of a judge was he, if he promoted Rustamov's stepson?

"I'm afraid we have had less time for collaboration with the schools, given the ongoing disruptions," he told the fourth judge, with all the cordiality he could muster.

"I understand completely. I won't detain you any longer."

They ended the call, still smiling, and then Emenev growled at the line of buses until he sounded like a one-man traffic jam. The fourth judge's sheer, undiluted entitlement was incredible. He hadn't even touched the tea that Umirvayet had sent over. Perhaps the Companies gave better gifts.

But the buses were still out there, oozing, waiting.

Emenev refused to go back into the depot without a solution. He was the judge who fixed things.

He outlined the problem in his mind, running it backwards and forwards like a legal brief. The expert system needed an authorization from the presiding judge; the fourth judge was presiding; the fourth judge did not care.

What gave the fourth judge this role? The Junpalto judicial division of authority, as represented by the contract all eight judges had negotiated between their offices and signed again when the first judge was sworn in.

But that wasn't the primary contract. The overarching rule was the emergency declaration, the one the fourth judge had insisted upon, that set the curfew and repurposed city supplies.

Bus tires were city supplies. Emenev wanted to repurpose them. All he needed was a writ. Nothing prevented him from issuing it immediately. Nothing, that is, save his utter lack of ribbons, authentication chips, or any of the other elements of an official document.

Emenev swept back into the depot office with the force of a prairie storm. It was close and dim after the courtyard with the buses. Emenev needed text, fabric shades, and scraps of code. A robot cut fabric into strips for him; another printed the official chips; the attendant unlocked the cabinet of expensive paper, fingers clattering against the metal door. In less than an hour, Emenev was reading the judicial ruling that created an override to his two human witnesses. They signed, the attendant's writing boxy and neat, the woman's brushed with horizontal trails that had been fashionable sixty years before. Just as important, each witness threaded a hastily painted ribbon through the hole punched for that purpose. Emenev tied the ribbons round the authorization chips and reasserted his ruling: "As seventh judge of the city of Junpalto, I set in abeyance the requirement for new winter tires, returning the buses to the streets."

His voice activated the chips and made the new rule official. The attendant bowed and took the document outside, putting it right back into the mailslot. But the expert system only needed the codes. Emenev geared up again to watch the robots restore his bus to working order, replacing the upgraded tires on the front and the old ones on the back. Then he used his tablet to request a ride back into the city. Since he and the woman with the umbrella represented the entirety of local bus demand, the bus was swiftly out front, waiting for them.

"Well, esteemed Mr. Judge!" the woman said. "You knocked some sense into that system. Thank you."

"This is the role of a judge. I do the work before me."

"We needed a person who cared. A person who could see how the machines were running wild, and make them stop. You did that all by yourself: you faced that system down and showed some human kindness. Take credit for it."

But Emenev had not acted by himself. He had followed the advice of a machine, the expert intelligence wrapped up inside his book. Kindness was crafted into it: that was the substrate shaping circuits into wisdom. "I rely on the insight of my friends, khaniet."

"That's right! Humans working together."

But not all of Emenev's friends were human.

THE WEEKS STRETCHED on; there was a day of flurries and a day of hail; the nights grew longer. There was a rumor that the Western Army was at the pass, and would arrive by Fifthday. There were better-substantiated rumors that the Lake Army was approaching; they were coming up the river; they were traveling by barge. Those rumors were confirmed by reports from the towns along the river, and then by a message from the general herself.

Emenev and the other judges went to the riverport to greet the army. The city's gold and silver banner rippled behind them; the breeze off the water drove strands of their wigs into their faces. The sixth judge had a heavy coat, with handwarmers stuffed in the sleeves. She still shivered.

Emenev wasn't cold. He felt the sharpness of hope, all the way down to the tips of his booted toes. The arrival of the Lake Army meant a return to ordinary problems, to Company lawsuits and requests from schools. When freight was flowing again, Kiza might return. He smiled at the late-flying geese on the river; he grinned at the shadow of an approaching barge.

As the barges came closer, he saw they were festooned with Lake blue. They had the round eyes of expert systems. But somebody had gashed those eyes, leaving a bold slash and artistic black droplets that might be tears, or blood. Emenev felt the drops like cold, cold water, weighing him down.

"This army. They're fanatics," he said aloud.

"In what sense?" asked the second judge. Everything the judges did was, ultimately, based upon divine harmonies, but she had no patience for religious enthusiasms.

"They believe humans must dominate, and expert systems be discarded."

"We could use more common, human sense," the fourth judge declared.

"It's our duty to chart the path for our fellow citizens," the eighth judge added. The sixth judge nodded vigorously.

Emenev had hoped for more sympathy—and more caution—from them both. "We must take care to preserve our rights and privileges," he said, hoping self-interest would protect where moral intuition failed.

"A fourfold balance has subsisted between the substantive components of society since the days our people roamed the deep," the third judge began.

Before Emenev could guide him, gently, to his point, the first barge was at the dock. The general strode toward them. Her pistol was at her waist; her guards held theirs in their hands. She and the judges traded bows.

They negotiated the surrender in a building made for wedding receptions and graduation parties, overlooking the river. Of course, they did not call it a surrender: it was an agreement for temporary disposition of forces. Emenev fought his customary battles. Curfew would not apply to delivery or retrieval of necessary food. The city kitchens would stay open. And the buses? They would still run, each with a soldier "supervising." Emenev shuddered, to think the general had a thousand spare people to ride buses; he hoped his response was hidden behind his beard and his customary judicial frown.

At last the substance of the agreement was complete. The colonels and the clerks were granted three hours to turn it into a physical document, complete with chips and ribbons. Emenev tucked an extra sky-blue ribbon in his pocket.

"And after the document is complete," the general said, "we will celebrate at the seventh judge's house. For you were the first to invite us, were you not?"

"This is a signal and unexpected honor, for this poor bachelor."

"I'll send a team ahead," the general said, her smile beneficent and unyielding.

Emenev took the bus back to his house: an odd episode of ordinariness, in an impossible day. He spent the ride messaging Umirvayet about caterers and portable heaters. His house was large, even luxurious, for a single person, but the judges and the general and her aides would have to spill into the courtyard. He reached home three quarters of an hour before the cleaning team.

He went upstairs at once and found the book. There was no disguising its importance, and not even silk and enamel could hide the fact that it was a machine. This was only a problem if the soldiers entered his bedroom— but of course they would check.

Emenev folded the book's silk beneath his pillow and pried its lock off with a table knife and a curse. He rubbed the rough edge with a bit of shoe polish to hide the glint, and ran his thumb around the other edges in apology. The book would understand. It strove for understanding, in a way Emenev only hoped to imitate.

He set his tablet to wipe itself and stuffed it in the kitchen junk basket: certain batteries and plastics needed special treatment. The book went into the breast pocket of his robes. They were thick enough to take the extra weight.

He still had time. His mother would have tidied, sweeping clutter into cupboards and behind curtains. But Emenev loved his house for its emptiness, the long bright spaces where he could stretch out alone, or sit with one particular friend. He had nothing else to hide. He went instead to the bathroom and trimmed his beard, letting the curls fall to the counter in heaps. The style made him feel like a singer, or a student working at a teashop over the holidays. There was more silver underneath the curls than he expected.

As his guests arrived, Emenev gathered their outer coats, carrying armfuls upstairs to lay across his bed. He swiftly ran out of guest slippers. The soldiers kept their boots on. That bothered him more than it ought, more than the cool directions of the cleaning team or the pistols at their belts. He set the feeling aside, on a high shelf in his mind that only he could reach, and dove into the duties of a host, proposing toast after toast. He had learned in his student days to pace himself, so he toasted with water and with cherry juice as well as vodka, and did not neglect the rolled sandwiches or the pistachio cakes. But he still felt warmth growing in the palms of his hands and the soles of his feet. He offered "Restful holidays!" to the second judge and "Smooth transit!" to the fourth. He drank to collaboration with a broadly smiling sergeant who had cake-crumbs in his mustache.

Emenev realized, as he set his empty glass down, that the sergeant's smile was forced. The man was staring at the broad sweep of his staircase with a questioning look Emenev recognized. He had worn the expression himself, staring into the fourth judge's rosewood-polished eyes and wondering, *How could something so beautiful belong to a person so spoiled?*

One had to know one's adversaries, as well as one's friends—perhaps better than one's friends—so Emenev asked, "Are you fond of architecture?"

The sergeant's false smile twisted into honest rue. "I thought I'd be an architect, once. Right up until a computer told me I was too piss-poor at poetry for a university student."

The toasts were affecting Emenev after all, because he asked the question in his head: "Your poetry scores were too low for the Faculty of *Architecture*? You didn't appeal?"

"Scraping by wasn't enough. My family needed my scholarship money—or I needed to join the army and plant wheat."

Emenev remembered that feeling—waiting for the scholarship funds to appear in his account, so he could buy his little brother a new tablet or find his sister a graduation scarf. The funds' arrival had always been approximate, give or take a week, for reasons he never understood. The university term always started on time.

But the situations were not parallel. A graduation scarf was hardly a necessity. "I see. You are a credit to your family."

"My kids will do whatever they want. Of their own choice. No exam-writing systems spinning out of some funeral pyre."

"Let's toast to your children. The next generation!"

The sergeant was still muttering about smoke and expert ghosts as Emenev slipped away, the book warm in its pocket against his chest.

Umirvayet and the general were in the courtyard, sharing a tray of vegetables. They had mushrooms roasted on skewers, radishes cut like flowers, and a stewfruit salsa.

Emenev was struck by how similar the two women looked: hands all vein and bone, eyes softened by shadow. They were discussing enhancements to the municipal water purification system. "You must designate a clerk for the final review," the general said.

"But do you not use expert systems in your own strategic planning?" Umirvayet asked.

"Notary-General Umirvayet, I am a different sort of general. The strategies I choose might mean war or famine. Those decisions must be made by the living."

"Because they know what is at stake?"

The general jerked her chin up and down. "Because they know what it means to die."

Umirvayet mirrored the nod, more slowly.

Emenev let the ebb and flow of the party carry him back towards the living room. He was not entirely inside before he heard the third judge suggesting, "Does it not happen, from time to time, that somebody continues to rely on the will of the algorithms, be it from sentiment, or customary procedure and habit, or even, though it pains me to include this possibility, simple laziness?"

"It's very simple," said his interlocutor. This soldier was built like a stack of rectangles. Her hair ribbon was new and crisp. "If somebody does not comply, then we take them outdoors, and we shoot them."

The third judge was already beginning to ask about due process. He was thorough, despite his prolixness: he would find the loophole, if there was one. Emenev was suddenly certain there was not. He slid back the sliding doors and went to find a glass of water.

In one of his least successful love affairs, Emenev had known a man whose family owned a cluster of cabins by a lake. They kept a collection of rifles in the largest cabin, ostensibly for hunting. In reality they were for sheer display, as impractical as an antelope's curving horns. Emenev's lover showed him how to grip the rifle, how to balance the weight and fire. It was heavy; it was lighter than he expected; it was too easy to curl his fingers round the trigger and hear the crack, its sound lessened by the earmuffs his lover wrapped around his head.

The pistol at the soldier's belt was not for display. She could lift it in one hand, wrap her fingers round it, pull the trigger back.

Terror rose in Emenev like the vodka's warmth, picking out the Lake-blue ribbons and obscuring his colleagues' robes. He had worried so much over Kiza, Kiza traveling, Kiza transformed. He had fretted and planned for the people of his city. But it had not occurred to him that he might, personally, be threatened.

He knew the threat would come. His book was not a secret: it was merely private. He could play the jovial host for now. But sooner or later the capsule description of him would dissolve, tincturing the army's knowledge of him: "devout but stubborn" would become "obsessed with the saints" and then "obsessed with the memories in the circuits of a book."

He could not protect the city if he left. But he could not protect the city if the soldiers walked him outside and shot him. It would happen in a single crack, like snapping a tablet screen in half. One learned very quickly, as a judge, that it was not difficult for a human to kill another human, if circumstance aligned.

Umirvayet had a rapport with the general. It would be possible for her to carry on the city's work. But if Emenev disappeared, he would not see Kiza again.

As Emenev came to this realization, the current of the party caught hold of him. There were latecomers to greet, some of the sixth judge's staff. He took their coats and toasted to their welcome. He did not choke on the vodka, though he was thinking of Kiza lost to him. He would be like a tidally locked moon-face, never reflecting the sun.

Emenev and Kiza had sworn no oaths and exchanged no ribbons. It was ridiculous, to stick upon this detail. It was ridiculous to have assumed that only Kiza could be lost.

Emenev took the newfound coats upstairs, and regarded the coats already there. Some of them were soldiers' overcoats. One or two were big enough to fit across his shoulders and button over his chest. He took the largest one and rolled it into the vacuum bag he kept for traveling. With the air sucked out, it curled like an immense centipede. He stuffed it into the top of his own voluminous sleeve, narrowly avoiding observation by a leytenant who was hunting for the upstairs bathroom.

Emenev spent a while in the clump of people by the downstairs bathroom, smiling indiscriminately and humming under his breath: "The goat shits in the mountains, the goat shits in the mountains, she leaves the seeds that grow the weeds that someday babies eat." His niece had loved that song, when she was a baby herself. He hoped she would still sing it when she was grown.

Emenev hummed the song twice through, then shrugged in vast frustration, tugged on his boots unlaced, and stomped to a half-lit patch of the outside wall. He pissed upon it for verisimilitude, wondering if the neighbors would object. None did.

He wandered idly down the block and around the corner to the unlit spot the neighbors always griped about. He stood a few minutes, looking up and down the street and letting the evening chill creep over him. He ran his fingers through his wig, feeling the strands part smoothly. Then he pulled it off, wrapping it into a package with the cap he wore beneath and the cords he'd braided for his professional associations and his siblings' children. There was no way to say goodbye, to explain why he had to shred the weaving. It might take decades for Simet to forgive him.

Emenev swapped his robes for the stolen coat and plaited his souvenir Lake ribbon into a single braid, as tight as he could make it. He shivered as the night wind found his scalp. But that could be solved by walking briskly. He caught a bus, stopped at a cash kiosk, caught another bus, and stopped at another kiosk, repeating until his pockets clinked with strings of chits and he stood before the arched doors of the intercity bus station.

Inside the station, an old man ate fried fava beans, letting a cleaning robot catch the crumbs, and a tiny person in an ankle-length coat napped on top of their luggage: that was all the passengers in the huge and echoing room. Emenev dropped chits into the chute of a machine till it spat out a ticket on the next route southwest. The destination was named Four Sheep Waiting. Fine print on the back of the ticket warned that in case of inclement weather, travel might be delayed for multiple days: Four Sheep was high in the mountains. But the night was cold and fair.

"Are you on leave, sir?" the old man asked, folding his snack packet and pressing it neatly.

"The first in a long time, khanik," he said, imitating the sergeant's hearty growl. "Forgive me, that's my bus."

Emenev sat in the high-backed seats, trying to maintain a soldier's posture. The lights were dim, the windows mirrored. The stops and turns of city streets ended; they began to climb. His eyes were gritty with exhaustion, but he wasn't ready to close them. He opened the book instead. It offered him verse:

THE PRAIRIE IS GUARDED BY WINDMILLS.
THEIR BLADES REVOLVE AS SLOWLY
AS THE MOTION OF THE STARS.
BELOVED, I ASK, WHERE ARE YOU?
YOU ARE THE WARMTH THAT TURNS THE WORLD.

That was strange comfort, Emenev thought, for a journey away from everyone he had ever known. But the turning of the bus wheels and the turning of the windmill blades overlapped in his mind, and then he was asleep.

He woke when someone took the seat beside him: a small man, with a fussy trailing headwrap, who balanced a huge orange rucksack on his lap. "You could place that in the rack above," Emenev began to say. It was the softest version of, "Take any seat but that one."

The man hugged the backpack and turned toward him. Something unfurled in Emenev. He hugged them both, the man and the pack, gripping, gripping, as if that water-sloughing orange fabric was the sun, drawing him in. The book's corner made a bruise above his heart. The man was Kiza.

"How?" Emenev asked, when they pulled apart enough for him to breathe.

"Your friend sent word," Kiza told him, with a nod toward the pocket where the book rested.

Emenev had spent so long wishing he knew the measure of Kiza's affection. Now all their braids were lies, yet Kiza's fingers were strong at the back of his neck, as if they could hold each other forever, crammed into two seats that made a world. He tried to kiss Kiza lightly, to give space, to allow for time, but Kiza bit his lip and he laughed and they curled tongues against tongues, wrapped up, pulled tight. His friend the book had spoken to his friend who was beloved. Emenev knew, then, that the warmth of his friends was infinite.

TEN PERCENT FOR LUCK

in the year 3312 of the Nakhorian reckoning

EVERYONE IN THE village had a rifle, and they all smiled too much. The aqmada was inside one of the houses, smiling back and drinking tiny glasses of tea. Zhanu Samayovet thought the leytenant should have gone with him. That wasn't right, though. The leytenant should *be* him: she should be Aqmada Inkar Alyevet, negotiating with the villagers, not Leytenant Alyevet, guarding a truck with Zhanu.

The bad news had trickled in slowly. Originally, the word was just that Alyevet was changing divisions. Then there were rumors that she'd run into some sort of trouble on leave. (Rumor said Company trouble, but the army usually kept away from Companies). Zhanu had thought hard, and left a dozen baursaqi, fried golden and sprinkled with rose syrup, at the green saint's shrine. Then she'd put in for a transfer. Rumors were one thing, but a good officer was another. Right now, though, Zhanu was just watching the smart truck, in case it got bored and started wandering. That gave her too much time to wonder which rumors had been true.

Most of the villagers pretended Zhanu and the leytenant were invisible, but an old woman walked right up to them. She was tall, though bent slightly with age, and her headscarf was embroidered with blue flowers. She carried two pistols at her waist instead of a rifle slung over her back, which looked like the elder's privilege of not giving a fuck. The woman stared down at Zhanu and said, "They didn't let you into the meeting either, huh?"

"Leytenant Alyevet and I are keeping the truck company, khaniet."

"And who are you, dear? The first leytenant?"

Zhanu glanced at Alyevet, worried. The woman shouldn't be talking to her at all. Even if you didn't recognize their insignia, Alyevet was so clearly the superior officer, poised and confident. Except that Zhanu's hair was braided with the divisional red and silver, while the leytenant's head was shaved like a new recruit's.

Alyevet cupped her hand very slightly, in the signal that meant, "I've got your back." Then she turned on the full force of her smile. Unlike the villagers' smiles, which implied if they stopped feeling pleased they would shoot you, Alyevet's grin was individual and genuine. "Khaniet," she said, "this is Sergeant Aruzhan Samayovet, an expert in explosive ordnance disposal. I am honored to be able to introduce her to you."

Alyevet was the real explosives expert. But that was nice of her to say.

"Well!" the woman answered. "I thought you people were more in the business of selling ordnance than disposing of it."

Alyevet bowed. "Mines kill soldiers, as well as farmers and sheep. And we have found that even safely stored ordnance poses problems. Somehow, when people have explosives, they find ways to use them."

"I expect you're also good at improvising explosives?"

"The skills are similar, khaniet," Alyevet admitted. "But in my experience, there are enough bombs around without our making new ones."

"If I told you where to find a cave full of ammunition, what would you do? Take it and keep it somewhere less tempting?"

"Khaniet, we would blow it up," Alyevet answered. "And destroy the cave entrance, to protect any wandering children, or goats." Unless the cave was conveniently located near a major highway under the army's control. But there weren't a lot of those, around here.

"Find a map, dear," the woman told Zhanu.

At a nod from Alyevet, Zhanu went around the far side of the truck to retrieve her slate. The door opened to her knock. Meanwhile, Alyevet was making polite noises about young people's irrational fears as a prelude to asking, "How would I know Vaikheti snipers wouldn't be waiting, on the way to such a cache?"

"I will tell my nephew not to send them!" the woman said, almost laughing. "But it doesn't matter if you believe me. Your commander will risk you, either way."

That was the formal reminder that the villagers weren't on the army's side, except when the army was useful to them. Zhanu felt sorry for this woman's nephew. "Here is the map, khaniet, sir," she said, so the leytenant wouldn't have to answer nicely. She held her slate where the others could see it and pulled up a tourist map. It didn't have the resolution of the military charts, and some of the listed towns weren't there any more, but the mountains were still in the right places.

Alyevet caught Zhanu's eye for a moment. She seemed approving. Then the leytenant and the village woman descended into a long, technical discussion involving streams, trails, high pastures, and the exact location of an artificial cave in the nearest mountain. The other villagers continued to stay away.

As the mapping conversation ended, Alyevet asked, "Khaniet, what do you gain from telling us this?"

"Would you believe I dream of prosperity and peace between our peoples?" the woman asked, still smiling. "An accord the friends of God would bless?"

"I would not contradict the wisdom of my elders, khaniet," the leytenant answered. Zhanu admired her ability to say so without apparent sarcasm. Alyevet had always been good at village politics, though. She remembered all the tiny, patchworked understandings that brought a unit vegetables and notice of springtime attacks.

"Your courtesy exceeds my nephew's!" said the woman. "He should have invited me to tea with your commander."

FLYERS COULDN'T LAND near the cave: the slope was too steep and the wind was too high. There wasn't enough of a road for trucks, either, not even smart ones. That gave Zhanu the whole five-hour hike up the mountain to wonder if the woman had been telling the truth, and if she should be here at all.

The squad of four moved in single file. Zhanu was at the rear, as was right and proper for a sergeant. The two soldiers in front of her were taller, but not so used to the altitude. Zhanu kept pace with them easily. Gulasova coughed sometimes (they'd picked up a bug in transit, as likely as not). Rayanev kept starting to whistle, and then realizing that was a bad idea. Zhanu would have to speak to him about the whistling. As the sun rose higher, she realized she'd have to mention his ribbons, too. The divisional silver and red braided into his queue was shiny new, too bright to look like flowers and too orange to be a bird. Zhanu had dipped her ribbons in tea, first thing after the transfer; Gulasova had flown in from another base, and their ribbons had the frayed ends of long use. Of course Alyevet didn't have a braid, and Zhanu didn't know why.

But here Zhanu was, catching glimpses of Alyevet at the front of the line. The leytenant was carrying a rifle and a bulky pack, like all the rest of them, and her mottled green coat hung loose. But she strode up the mountain as if it was a meadow. Zhanu imagined her watching the path ahead, winged brows just slightly drawn together. Alyevet had beautiful ears, with the defined, almost pointed lobe that would show a pair of earrings to perfection. And that sort of thought, right there, was why everyone else assumed Zhanu had transferred divisions. All the stories pointed one way: the general and his boon companion, the khanym and her sworn sister...but Zhanu had served under Alyevet for three good years. If anything was going to happen between them, it would have started ages ago. What mattered was that Alyevet could talk to people, and knew things about rocks.

The cave was more or less where the village woman had claimed. At first it looked just like an opening where rock had washed out, under a rivulet. But there was a crack they could thread a wire through, with a camera and a light. That showed a corridor, about the height and width of a person, with stacks of boxes down the right-hand edge. The cross section looked like one bubble on top of another, which meant the tunnel had been cut in haste with a couple of borer drones.

The boxes would be full of explosives. Zhanu chiseled
the hole wider, until they could tilt the disc drone from
Gulasova's pack sideways and send it in to make a map.
Meanwhile, Rayanev moved about downslope, setting grav
sensors to gauge how far the system extended. The sensors
were finicky. Rayanev had to dig each one a little way into
the earth, and then walk away a couple meters so as not
to skew the readings. Zhanu's old team had joked that one
interfering family of marmots could wreck an entire squad.

Alyevet had her slate out, and was sketching where to
set the charges. They needed to destroy as much of the
weapons cache as they could, and collapse enough of the
tunnel system to prevent the Vaikheti from retrieving the
rest. She worked quickly and calmly, integrating the data
from Rayanev and the drone as it came in. Zhanu kept
an eye on her watch. They needed to get back down the
mountain and call for a flyer before the sun set.

Finally Alyevet flipped the slate around, and Zhanu
started checking her work. The big question was how far
down the mountain to stand, to avoid being hit by flying
debris. On flat ground, and if you knew the all-up weight
of the explosives you were working with, the equation
was simple. Here, which mountain you were on mattered,
since tunnels in some rock would collapse and others just
focused the explosions. And the weight was always a bit of
an estimate.

"I'll send the trigger command," Alyevet said. That
would put her closest to the blast.

Zhanu nodded, still checking. The leytenant was reliable,
but procedures were procedures. And indeed, the placements
all made sense. Rayanev's measurements said they had to
place one charge out and to the side, to collapse a tunnel
spur, but everything else seemed standard. Except—"You
didn't add ten percent, sir." They always stood back a little
further than the computations required, just in case.

Alyevet said, "That is correct, sergeant."

Zhanu made the change. Then they were all in motion, retrieving sensors, setting charges, stuffing gear back into packs for the long hike down.

It wasn't until they had watched the hillside shudder in on itself, till a rock the size of Zhanu's two fists had bounced and settled a meter away, that Zhanu registered the leytenant's tone. She hadn't meant, "Fix it." She'd meant, "You're right."

THE NEXT EVENING, after supper, Zhanu went to the leytenant's office. Alyevet controlled half of a round, temporary building. The sides were canvas, but the door was set into a solid wood frame. Zhanu knocked, and waited. Eventually, the leytenant shouted, "Come in!"

Equipment was stacked close to the office walls: pressure plates, grav sensors, vibration sensors, boxes of ammunition. Alyevet's shoes were set next to the doorway. The main light came from a portable lantern on her desk. The white glow of her slate illuminated her face and glinted off the residue of gold polish on her nails. "I want you to know," Alyevet said, "you can leave at any time."

Zhanu was nonplussed. If the leytenant didn't want her there, she wouldn't have let her in. "Sir. I wanted to ask you—"

"You followed me. You changed divisions." The leytenant stood, and set both hands on Zhanu's shoulders.

Zhanu looked up, into her odd, black-ringed eyes. When the leytenant kissed her, it felt both inevitable and unreal. They both started out trying to kiss slowly, thoughtfully. But they shifted almost immediately into quick, hungry kissing, biting each other's lips.

"Do you want this?" the leytenant asked, pulling away
for a breath.

"Sir, I never believed *you* would want—"

Alyevet traced the bones of Zhanu's face with lightly
curled fingers. Around her eyes, her cheeks. "You are
allowed to ask for things for yourself."

But Zhanu wasn't just some sort of token cast onto
a map. She wanted things in relation to other people.
What she wanted now was to know what the leytenant
was doing. If Alyevet had a plan at all, or if she was just
spinning, striking the edges of the world harder and
harder, until something felt like enough.

When Zhanu asked the question like that, the answer
seemed obvious. Zhanu couldn't steady the leytenant
on her own. You never could make that choice for other
people. But she didn't want to walk away, either. "I do
want you, here, with me. Sir."

The leytenant kissed Zhanu's forehead, and beside her
eye. "You know," she said, "I'm Nazhka, to my friends."
That sarcastic grin meant, maybe, "if I have any left."

Zhanu tried it, in her head: Nazhka Alyevet and Zhanu
Samayovet, in an office, fraternizing. Kissing. But the
diminutive felt wrong, too childish for the woman she'd
known mostly as Aqmada Inkar Alyevet. Could she think
just the first name? Inkar? "Inkar," she said, aloud this
time, touching the slightly spiky fuzz of hair at the nape of
the leytenant's neck.

In response, Inkar unsnapped Zhanu's coat, pushing
it open. In the process, her hand brushed Zhanu's breast.
Zhanu sucked in her breath, trying to stay quiet. Nobody
was working in the other half of the office, not this time
of night, but the walls were still canvas. Inkar tugged up
Zhanu's tunic and untwisted the clasp at the front of her
bra. Zhanu sighed, softly. The leytenant's fingers were a
little bit cold, and it was so easy to focus on them touching
her breast. Hands cupped, thumb circling.

But it wasn't fair, just to feel. Zhanu pulled at Inkar's
coat. The leytenant took it off, folded it, then crossed her
arms and pulled her tunic over her head in one smooth
motion. Her breasts were bare, pointed, her nipples large.
Zhanu wanted to trace them with her tongue, to nibble.
But instead, Inkar reached for Zhanu's belt, unhooked
it, and slipped her hand inside Zhanu's pants. Her finger
brushed Zhanu's clit, but it was too much, too bright. Zhanu
was glad when it slipped inside her, instead. She rested her
head on Inkar's shoulder and felt herself held, the pressure
of the heel of Inkar's hand, her fingers moving. Zhanu shut
her eyes and tried not to squeak, not to breathe. She let the
tension of her fingers on Inkar's bare skin say yes, now, more.
Then she was warm and sleepy, all at once, and smiling.

Zhanu drew back very slightly and looked for the coats.
Inkar's was folded neatly on the desk. There was just
enough clear floor space to lay it out, like a blanket. Zhanu
found her own coat and rolled it loosely, then draped the
leytenant's tunic over, to form a makeshift pillow. She
thought she'd lay Inkar down, take off her trousers, and kiss
down along her body. But instead she found herself lying
on her back, Inkar's knee between her legs, teeth biting
her neck. Zhanu pushed against Inkar's knee, against the
hands stroking her breasts. It wasn't right just to accept, to
feel. But it was so easy to go where the leytenant sent her,
to be hers in all the small motions of her body. This time,
when Inkar touched Zhanu's clit, she wanted to bask in the
brightness, to stretch that moment out forever.

Inkar's hand was still resting inside Zhanu's pants,
comfortable and warm, a little later. "What was it you
wanted to ask me, earlier?"

Zhanu couldn't ask about safety margins for explosives,
not here. Instead she said, "Why are we doing this now?"

Inkar laughed, the sort of startled, overwhelming laugh
that comes when things are falling apart. "Because I fucked
up. They told us, in training, that if we were any good at

all, some of our people would want us. That it wasn't truly
personal, and wouldn't last. I knew you liked me, but—I
didn't think it mattered. And now it does."

Leytenant logic wasn't, as the saying went. Seemed like
that still held true, the second time around? Zhanu wrapped
her arms around Inkar and held her tight for a good, long
minute. Then she rolled them sideways and pulled away a
bit, starting to sit up.

"You're not leaving?" Inkar asked, voice small.

"I want to take my boots off!" Zhanu fumbled at the laces
and tugged off her boots by the heels. Then she kneeled and
removed Inkar's trousers. The leytenant's hips were narrow.
It was easy to undress her, easy to keep her warm with lips
and mouth. Inkar took to the silence naturally, it seemed. It
was just the slowness of her hips, the relaxation of her hand
on Zhanu's braid, that said when she was done.

Zhanu stretched her body out against the leytenant's,
feeling the roughness of her own tunic, and tasting sweet and
salt together. After a while, she asked, "How did you come
to join the army?" That was the sort of question you asked
when you were on leave in the city with someone. Several
toasts into the evening. It felt strange to ask it sober. But it
also felt strange not to know.

"My family were all in Otter Company," said Inkar.

"Otter, like rivers? Canals?" Were the rumors about
Company trouble true, then?

"Yes, rivers, canals, roads. My auntie showed me how
to blast out a mountain pass, using firecrackers in the
sandbox. We were that kind of family."

"But why the military?" Because it sounded like Inkar
hadn't just taken a contract with Otter Company. Her
parents might have had actual shares. People with that
sort of income didn't join up, usually, not even with a paid
commission.

"Because I wanted to build something." Inkar ran her
hands down Zhanu's braid. Her hand settled in the small of

Zhanu's back, where her tunic was pushed up.

"Don't Companies build things?"

"For themselves. So they can take the tolls. The army, we protect everyone. It doesn't matter who you are, or if you know both parents' names."

That was a Company-brat way to think. They were the ones who cared about lineages, shares, and legal ceremonies. Or didn't care, in the leytenant's case. "So we're building big holes in the sides of mountains."

"Only the best!" Inkar pulled on Zhanu's hair, gently, as she wove her fingers through the ribbon at the end of the braid.

Zhanu was ready to stop talking. She lifted her head.

EIGHT DAYS LATER, the squad was riding a smart truck at the head of a tiny convoy. The road was mostly ruts and dried-out stream bed, but the truck was smart enough to find a path. That meant the four soldiers could brace themselves against the jolts, and watch the hillsides. These hills had lots of towers, old ones, made of light stone with gray slate roofs. Whoever was here first had money, to program the cutters to fit all that stone. The people here now had sheep. Zhanu watched for motion, or shining metal. She ended up aiming at a lot of white fleece.

One of those towers was up ahead, a big square one. There were sheep in the road, too, including a ram with big curling horns. "Sir—" Zhanu said.

Inkar was already on the radio, yelling at the other trucks to pause, keep distance, go around. Zhanu looked for people in the tower. That meant she didn't see whatever bit of debris the truck crunched over. She felt the shaking, though, the rattle through all of her bones as the explosion hit. Somewhere a sheep baaed, like a person shouting.

"Damage exceeds self-repair tolerance," the truck said plaintively. "Manual repair required." Meanwhile there was a series of pops from the towers. Definitely people with rifles there, shooting from the old arched windows. The louder crunch was a grenade.

"Go, go, go!" Inkar yelled. "This is the kill zone!" Gulasova and Rayanev were already out the downhill doors and scrambling down the hillside. But Inkar wasn't leaving. She had a hatch up and was rummaging for the repair kit. She was going to lie under the truck and patch it herself.

"Sir. Someone has to cover you."

"Eight fucking hells. Sergeant." The leytenant had the kit now, though. She rolled out Gulasova's door and under the truck.

Zhanu crouched in the cab and watched the tower. The other trucks had pulled away. The sheep were gone, or dead. There was just the slow occasional crack, and then silence. The ambush was just a few village people, maybe. A few village people with a lot of explosives. Maybe the leytenant would have been all right, on her own?

There was a blur on the left, a smudge in the grasses on the hillside. It shifted right, coming closer. Zhanu fired. Either she'd frozen it in place, or she'd missed.

Zhanu heard a pop and a crack, as something hit plastic behind her. The grass shivered. That was very close range.

Zhanu yelled, "Stealther, incoming!" and set her rifle aside. She drew her pistol, laying down fire. Under the truck, the leytenant would have a knife. A few meters away, the blur paused. Then the grasses seemed to rip apart, and Zhanu saw a shirt, blood.

"Manual repair complete," the truck reported.

The leytenant climbed back into the cab. The door slammed. "We need the body. Grab it, let's go."

If anyone was still in the tower—But it was quiet now. Zhanu cracked open an uphill door, dropped out, and groped for the body's ankles. Genuinely a dead weight. But it paid to have a low center of mass, sometimes. She shoved the body back up into the cab, with the leytenant pulling. The truck was already grinding into motion again.

Zhanu climbed up and settled back into position, holding her rifle. The leytenant had a knife out. She stripped off the attacker's blurry coat, his mask. He'd covered his hair; of course, he wasn't proper military. He had the scraggly beginnings of a beard.

Zhanu started to ask, "Are there any—"

"I didn't give you permission to speak."

The body, naturally, was also silent.

It took three hours to reach the next base. They worked through all the check-offs and reporting. Somebody took away the body. They stowed their gear. Then Alyevet said, "Sergeant, follow me." Zhanu went after her, three steps behind. The leytenant hadn't been issued an office, yet. Instead, they found the exercise track, and stood at the center of the oval. Dusk was just starting to fall. The gray rocks shone a little in the fading light.

The leytenant set her hands on Zhanu's shoulders again, gripping hard this time. She didn't quite shake her. "You disobeyed my direct order."

"You would have died there, and sent the truck on without you."

"He almost shot you, sergeant."

"I'm protecting you. Sir." Even if that wasn't what the leytenant wanted. If it was the complete opposite.

The leytenant shook her head, too quickly. She should have had a braid, weighting her down.

"Sir, what are you doing?"

The leytenant unzipped one of her coat pockets and pulled out a silver disk. "The enemy had this, on his hat."

"Is it related to that village, somehow?"

"No. Look at it."

Zhanu took the jewelry. It had a pin back, and a design in relief. She tilted it, trying to catch the light. "This looks like one of the charms they sell for the green saint. But I don't see vines."

"It's for Navyai. One of the friends of God." The leytenant's voice was tight.

Zhanu waited. City people didn't care about the friends of God, usually. But all the mountain villagers did. Every soldier knew not to touch their shrines. This didn't explain why the leytenant was angry, or had almost gotten herself killed.

"We're too far south," the leytenant said. "You shouldn't have the cult of Navyai here. Unless something happened."

"Did something happen? Sir?"

"They're building a road." Uninflected, furious.

"Who is, sir?" But there was only one answer that made sense. The leytenant's family. Otter Company.

"I was home on leave when the proposal came out. I looked at the map. They're going to start with one of the pilgrimage routes and just level it out, cut straight through the mountain. Delete their shrine. We're going to lose thirty years of relationship-building." Some of which was Alyevet's. All those careful, smiling conversations in all those little tiny villages.

"You told your family what the army would think?"

"My family was bidding on *a military fucking contract*."

Politics. Companies and politics. And a general, somewhere, who wanted more people to kill. "What did you do?"

"I painted my nails and I covered my hair and I went to the shareholders' meeting. I warned them our crews would be taken out by religious zealots."

Alyevet was a good officer. She had been before that, probably, a favored daughter of her Company. She expected people to welcome and approve her. "They didn't listen?"

"They asked the army for a hazard bonus."

Zhanu reached out and touched the leytenant's arm. She didn't react in any obvious way, but she didn't push Zhanu away, either.

"Then I got an invitation to tea with the polkovniki. He told me soldiers don't hide their braids, and if I wanted to vote Company shares, I could resign my commission."

"And you told him you wouldn't?"

"I told him I didn't have a family."

Oh, Inkar. Zhanu's hand tightened. The leytenant must have sounded just that certain when she was talking to the polkovniki. It was one of the basic skills of command, sounding like you believed exactly what you were saying. But you couldn't shift your superior officers just by being sure. Inkar should have known that. She knew how to nod, and half-agree, and maneuver people slowly. But maybe she hadn't believed she should need that skill, with someone who ought to be on her side already?

"The polkovniki told me I had a problem with listening. That perhaps I'd focus better with a change of scene."

If she'd been talking to another sergeant, Zhanu would have cursed the pigheadedness of commissioned officers, and offered to buy the next round. The leytenant wasn't ready to joke about wrongs done to her yet, though. She was only just barely talking at all. "So here we are?" Zhanu asked.

"So here we are."

"Do you know, sir," Zhanu said, "lots of people aren't army or Company. You could resign this commission, and go to the city. Do something different. Teach geology, maybe."

"You wouldn't be there."

"I could follow you, sir." It was getting dark. The track lights had motion sensors. They'd start glowing if either Inkar or Zhanu moved. But right now they were both still.

Inkar reached for Zhanu's right hand, and took the pin from her. "Or I could stay here, and build things. I know how to do that. Shrines and all."

"You might need to be higher ranked than a leytenant." Which would entail staying alive long enough to get promoted.

"You might need to listen better than I do!" There was part of a laugh in the leytenant's voice, now.

Inkar shifted toward Zhanu. Their shoulders touched. The lights snapped on. But Zhanu could wait. She could move slowly. She could hold Inkar, as night fell, in a temporary oval of darkness.

THE ASSOCIATION OF TWELVE THOUSAND FLOWERS

in the year 3370 of the Nakhorian reckoning

I SEE THE green and lilac ribbon braided tight and tucked under the brim of your hat. Thanks for the confirmation—you could call it an installment payment. My part of our bargain is this story.

My story begins on a lovely night, one of those clear crisp early-summer evenings where the sun lingers well into working hours but the cool air begs for a silken wrap or a shot of vodka. I got off the tram at the edge of downtown and unbuttoned the top of my coat. Each button was shaped like a round peony bud, and the opening framed the soft skin of my neck. I glanced down, judged the effect good, and traced a squiggle on my tablet to summon a velokab.

A kab came right away, which I thought meant good luck. It was painted with shiny yellow enamel, and the driver, a woman maybe a decade or two older than me, had a bright yellow headscarf to match. I was just about to swing into the seat behind her when she said, "I don't give rides to bastards."

"Do I know you?" I was genuinely wondering if I had slighted her somehow. I meet so many people, with so many faces.

"I'm seeing you." Her gesture took in my sheer tunic, my flowing veil. "You'll have never known a contract."

I could hear the traces of her high-mountain accent now, the way she hopped from vowel to vowel without intervening consonants to smooth the introductions. She meant 'bastard' literally, that I was a child of one parent, born without a lineage. And the mother of future bastards, presumably. As if—may every face of the green saint witness me—I didn't know how contraception worked.

I stroked her right hand gently, where it rested on the open dash. "Don't worry. I would have hired you to drive me for an hour, but I won't now. You'll have to find another *very short-term* contract."

She stomped on the pedals. Her velokab lurched forward, straight toward a tourist hugging an overstuffed duffel. The tourist dropped their bag. I started to scream. But the velokab's sensors cut in and jerked sideways, sliding the kab into traffic a hand's-breadth behind a fat gray truck.

I watched the kab drive away, bobbing and turning through the traffic like a candy wrapper floating down the river. I made myself relax my toes and my fingertips. I thought about breezes on water. But my breath was still knotted up like a Company contract. I had almost stolen somebody's life, because she hurt my feelings.

You're shaking your head. You wouldn't hold me to account. The judges wouldn't either, no matter how smug they are, in their snow-white wigs. That's what kab drivers are for: to be responsible. A velokab can more or less pilot itself. But machines can't make moral choices. Or strategic ones either, supposedly. That's why, if a kab ever crashes, its driver is supposed to pay the price.

When people talk about humans taking responsibility, they always seem to mean somebody else.

The next kab I summoned was driven by my friend Talga, and if I could have jumped over the dash, I would have hugged them. I settled for a heartfelt handclasp and a distracting question: "How's business?"

They pulled away from the curb with a satisfied little whistle. "All charged up!"

Any city resident gets a power allowance, but it's not enough to run a kab on, no matter how hard you pedal. If you don't have a connection to a Company or one of the judges' charities, you're stuck paying surge prices. Or, if you're smart like Talga, you siphon power.

They told me about a lunch counter just on the other side of the river that sold high-mountain food, stacks of pancakes filled with onion and pumpkin and fried in lots of butter. The owner was obsessed with endurance bike racing. He probably made as much from bets as from his pancakes, no matter how crispy they were. The whole back wall of the restaurant was devoted to a race display, with mountain paths molded in real time and toy bikes creeping along. Except cliffs kept popping up, and disappearing. Talga debugged the display, and in return the owner let them park. Their velokab charged while the restaurant was closed.

We drove for a while, past kiosks selling tourist scarves and restaurants with rooftop grills. Many people smiled once at me, but nobody glanced twice. A cold voice in the back of my mind started doing arithmetic about fares and rent.

Talga asked, "How is your situation, really?"

I should have known that they would recognize I was deflecting. "I met a kab driver who hates all twelve thousand of us flowers."

I would have said more, but near the next corner, music was blaring from a basement teahouse. A woman with a zigzag headscarf leaned against the stairway railing, looking back and forth between her tablet and the sky. I asked Talga to go a little slower.

"Saved by a prospect, huh, Rauzanet?" But they brushed their hand along the dash, and the kab obeyed.

The woman's jacket looked like Company issue: it was short and severe, except for the brightly embroidered patch over her heart. The orbital station would be visible beyond the skyscrapers, despite our light pollution, so maybe she was watching for it. Or maybe she was afraid a piece of skyscraper would fall on her. She had the twitchy look and slightly hunched shoulders of someone who spends a lot of time underground, or watching underground cameras. A miner, or a mining engineer. Either way, a likely customer.

I tapped the long handle of my fan against the edge of the kab door, metal ringing against metal. The woman glanced up. I held her gaze for a long moment, smiling like we shared a tiny, private joke, and then shook my head and let my gauzy veil fall across part of my face. Traffic was moving again, but Talga swung the kab round the corner without me having to ask. The trefoil vine charm above their head swung wildly.

Talga's tablet chimed with a shared-ride request before we were halfway around the block. I laughed. Slow night, yeah, but I was still a star. Because here's the thing. The back of a velokab can fit two living creatures, if one of them is a sixteen-year-old in the throes of first love, or a kitten. If you're old enough to form a binding contract and you're requesting a shared ride, you're not looking to save a couple of coins, you're looking for someone like me.

Once we were back on the teahouse corner, I set my fan on the seat—it had suggestive illustrations—and swung the kab door open. The woman took my hand and helped me alight. I felt like a khanym's mistress alighting from a star-ferry, in some ancient tale.

She kept holding my hand as she said, "Will you tell me, are you part of a larger firm?"

That was not only auspicious, but interesting. Most people are anxious about the price of my services—but this woman was asking about privacy.

I told her, "I am a sole proprietor," and watched her shoulders relax. "I even have a data security expert on retainer." My security expert is also my girlfriend, but that was more information than she wanted.

"It sounds like an impressive operation!" Her thumb traced the base of my thumb, tentative.

I shook my head with a tiny bit of self-deprecation, letting my veil slip back from my face, and knew by the skip in her breathing that our deal was complete.

My new client fired off a message to her friends, who were still drinking in the teahouse. Then I packed her into the velokab, promising Talga would look after her. They smiled. It was their smile for guests and customers, lower lip hiding the edges of their teeth, but it was genuine, for all of that. As the kab pulled away, I heard them asking my client whether she was in a traditional field, such as nephrite or diamonds, or did she source materials for the station? Either way, Talga would welcome her and tell her stories about the city. They would also make sure she didn't find another amusement, between the teahouse and my workspace: if you weren't careful, sometimes clients wandered off for another drink. I waved a cheerful, temporary goodbye, and caught the next velokab.

We pulled up by the old terraced house that held my workspace a minute or so behind Talga and my client. Sometimes I brought clients in through the lift around back, but this time I unlocked the door with the charm on my bracelet and led her up the narrow stairs. I glanced back once. Her eyes were wide and dark, wider even than you'd expect in the dim passageway.

I was proud of my workspace. A screen covered one wall with shifting golden tracery, sometimes a network of neurons, sometimes a network between stars. Light fanned out above the bed, with its rich blue coverlet. Talga had helped me with the wiring. A shorter lamp sat on a table, beside the low couch and the samovar ready with tea.

I drew my client inside and kissed her, fiercely, like I was the one who was hungry, like I was a ship and she was the gateway to the Deep. She laughed in the back of her throat and held me close, shivering a little with the tightness of her grip. But a minute later she asked, "Is there a contract? I don't—I haven't done this before."

Maybe she hadn't. Maybe she had, but didn't want to believe this was a habit. It wasn't my business. I guided her to the couch instead, and offered her tea or vodka. She chose tea. I poured vodka for myself, in a tiny crystal glass. This was a double strategy: to make her feel relaxed, as if we were continuing the teahouse party together, and to make her a little guilty for not matching me toast for toast. It's always useful, when a client thinks they owe you something extra.

The contract was on a handheld screen, a nice one, its back embossed with diamond tiles. My default term was two hours. The client promised not to disparage my services or seek information about my other clients. I promised confidentiality, in the old language: *I will not communicate what I know or guess about your bindings, in speech, writing, or by gesture, to any being living or emulating life, so long as our own lives endure.*

The signature page was a mirror. My client looked at it, still wide-eyed, and seeming more so from the lightness of her brows. The screen collapsed her face to an impenetrable hash, a dappled pattern of shadow and light. I gave it my own face in turn. Then I took her hand, and we went toward the bed.

Our first motions were rushed, her fingers on my nipple, her leg trapped between mine as she rocked against my hand. It was only after all the tension was shaken out of her, in a series of half-laughing warbling cries, that she ran her fingers through my hair. The strands slipped freely. There was just one narrow, heavier braid weighted by my Aid Collective ribbon, reflective tape backed by midnight blue. Meanwhile, my client had lost a hairpin somewhere. Her zigzag-patterned scarf was pushed back, and the plain kerchief underneath was slipping, showing the braids at her temple. I liberated the remaining pins. She made a little huffing sound, the kind of noise you make when you're working up the nerve to do something frightening, and pulled both scarves off.

I kissed her temple and her eyelids, letting her feel the protection of our bargain, letting her grow calm. "It has been a long time?"

"Half a year, on this assignment. Another half-year, before I can go home."

She was married, of course. I had guessed that from her age and her Company insignia, and known it the moment her kerchief slipped, showing a flicker of yellow. She had the brilliant purple cords of an Amaranth Company employee, too. She was only an employee, not a shareholder. A shareholder wouldn't have had to spend a year away from her children, and I saw the copper ribbons for two children, braided at the nape of her neck.

There was another ribbon I didn't recognize, a jaunty spiral of lilac and green twisting above her right ear. She could push back her scarf with one hand and display that promise, the way you did. I had learned more about her; I'd seen all her obligations. But then, she knew I was bound, despite my lack of braids. As long as our own lives endured.

I wouldn't be telling you this story, if it wasn't for that clause.

I held her, and we talked. Not about anything close to her heart, or at least, nothing that seemed so at the time.

More about colors of jade. It was a light shade that was most valuable, a kind that seemed thick and soft, like wax. Like the fat from cardamom pastries, she told me. It seemed like, if you wrapped the jade pieces up in paper, it would turn translucent. The miners sent mechanical snakes into the ground hunting jade, snakes with bright lamps and teeth sharp with cheap factory diamond. Their tails dragged the network cable that told them where and how to hunt. But the snakes' eyes caked with grit, and the cable snagged and broke, and the Company wouldn't fund replacements or improvements, not for an engineer who didn't own a single share. So it was personal money or personal time, stretching all your attention underground, till you forgot who you were or what bound you to the surface.

"You could be eight repeaters," she told me, "or twelve lamps."

I laid a sharp line of kisses from the base of her ear to the base of her neck, and asked her to interpret the signal, and then we were done talking for a while.

I saw my client back to Talga's kab, when her contracted time was up, and then took a moment to straighten my workspace and rearrange my veil. I was just thinking about going out again when my tablet chimed with her tip. It was a tidy sum. Four lamps, by her exchange rate, or a string of jade beads, gleaming like drops of oil. I didn't think I could do better, with the late crowd. I debated for a few minutes. At last I shrugged, changed into my off-duty scarf, and caught the second-to-the-last tram back to my girlfriend's place. Khoshet was already asleep when I arrived, twirled up in the quilts like a boy in his first turban. I liberated one corner, and curled around her, and fell fast asleep.

I WOKE TO the sound of my tablet buzzing on the floor beside the mattress. A burst of vibration, and then silence, and then another burst. I didn't understand why the room was still dark. Calls shouldn't come through, if the room was still dark. I stabbed at the tablet, and keyed, "Who?"

I saw Talga's icon, the triple vine, and the insistent pulse of their demand for a voice call.

I wrapped myself in a quilt and took the call on the other side of the room, by the kitchen nook. I wasn't offering visuals, but Talga was. There were a couple of beetle-sized lights beside them, but the main illumination came from their screen. Their cheek was scraped, and their turban was askew. I couldn't see their kab.

"I'm out back, by your lift. I need you to let me in."

"Talga, I'm at Khoshet's."

They shook their head. This was one fact too many. "So bring her. Rauzanet, please. I'll be all right. I just—I just need a cup of tea."

They were lying. I didn't know how or why or who had hurt their face, but they were exhausted. Tendrils of dark hair fell across their forehead, where their turban was slipping. "We'll be right there."

In the end, it took a quarter of an hour for me to drag Khoshet into consciousness, and another half-hour for us to walk over, with the tram lines quiet. Talga's kab wasn't parked out front, and I wondered at first if they had gone somewhere else, but when we walked around the building they were there, slumped back against the wall like they had gone to sleep standing up. Their left sleeve was ripped, and the mark on their face was blood.

"What happened?" Khoshet asked.

Talga shoved themself off the wall and took a step, grimacing. "I was afraid, if I sat down, I wouldn't be able to stand back up."

We took them up the lift, their arm over my shoulder, and put a blanket around them. I washed their face and brushed them off. Their clothes and turban were covered with fibrous splinters. Meanwhile, Khoshet made tea with extra sugar.

Talga stared at their glass as if they'd forgotten how to drink. "I saved these." They fished in their breast pocket and produced two objects. One was the threefold vine charm, from above their dash. The other was a flat gray cone, about the size of my thumbnail.

"Fucking thorns. Your license."

Talga giggled at me, in that high bleak way that's the other side of crying, and clutched the blanket around themself, and finally managed, "Yes."

The kab license was inside the charm. Oh, sure, it looked fragile. And this one was in the image of an icon for the Saint of Vines. But all the data was inside: the registration, Talga's right to pick up passengers, and all the images collected over the last year of sudden turns and shifts and stops. You would need clippers that could cut through diamond, to retrieve that charm when the kab was running. If Talga had it in their pocket, then their velokab was wrecked, and with it their livelihood. The gray cone looked like a sensor, but I didn't know where it was from.

I nudged the sugar bowl toward Talga, willing them to drink. Instead, they stared at me, clutching my deep blue throw in both fists. "She's dead."

"Who is?" But I could already feel the sadness stuck inside my chest, like a glass of tea too hot to finish swallowing, gulped too deep to spit out. Talga meant my client, the one who went drinking without filling in her eyebrows first, and told stories about snakes with diamond teeth. The one with copper ribbons for two children whose names I didn't know. Whose own name I didn't know. All I had was an account number, and the dappled pattern to encapsulate her face. That wouldn't matter, in the ordinary course of things. But in the ordinary course of things, my clients don't wind up dead.

Talga blinked slowly and finally sipped their tea. "There should be a recording of the bad parts, on the charm for the saint." They were slipping into their childhood voice, with the overly precise forms of an unwanted Company kid, drilled by tutors on some other continent.

"I've got it." Khoshet unfolded her notebook and coaxed it to interface with the charm, making soft shushing noises.

The recording opened on a long block flanked by skyscrapers. A delivery van was parked half on the pedestrian walkway and half on the street. We saw the flash of a logo, white catkins hanging from a branch, and then the van broke open. The back gate fell down, and the side walls too, crashing flat like toppled gaming tiles.

My client said something. Maybe "Shit." The recording wasn't optimized for sound.

"That's 'Trigger'," Talga whispered. On the recording, they dragged their shoulders into a desperate swerve. The van was too close, even with the kab's reflexes. The metal wall slammed onto the canopy. The kab spun and smashed. We heard a long, drawn-out crunch as the velokab's struts and bars crumpled around Talga. The kab frame was designed to take the force of a crash, and protect the passengers.

But the passenger had been thrown free. She lay half in the street and half on the far walkway. Talga moved toward her. In the charm's now-skewed perspective, they were all legs and shadow.

"Her scarf was still in place, Rauzanet. Her head was flopping, and I knew it wouldn't matter if I moved her, she was gone. But her scarf was perfect."

"I pinned it up for her." I bumped shoulders with Khoshet, to feel her presence. On her notebook screen, the recording cut to black.

Talga pressed their fists against their eyes. "I thought I could at least get the ramps out of the street, keep someone else from running over them, but the panels were locked open. I found that little gray cone while I was scrabbling for a hold."

Khoshet poked at it. The base still bore the marks of dried adhesive.

"Then I started walking. I didn't want my face to show up on a tram monitor." Or maybe they couldn't bear the thought of getting into another kab. Talga told us about the hike, out of downtown and over the bridges. The few people they passed looked the other way. They felt their feet puff up with blisters, and the blisters burst. Their recitation trailed off here.

"Talga, will a hunter be looking for you?" Khoshet spoke gently, but she was mapping out the danger. Legally, Talga was at fault. That's why kabs have drivers, right? A human has to be at fault, when somebody is killed.

Talga spread their hands in uncertainty. "Maybe? Our customer, was she married?"

I nearly snapped at Talga for their rudeness, and then I remembered she was dead. "She was married, and they had children." I was still working through the ramifications. "But she took a year-long contract here, without them. I don't think they can afford a hunter."

Talga was still trying to be logical. "What about Amaranth Company? She was Amaranth, right?"

A Company could certainly pay. I winced and offered them a hand as anchor.

"Amaranth won't investigate."

We both looked at Khoshet.

She spun her tablet and showed us two images. The first was as she had reconstructed it from Talga's footage: those white catkins against a black circle, painted on the side of the van, a little scuffed. The second was the logo of an Amaranth subsidiary, the same circle and catkins, with the subsidiary's name in flowing script. "So you're safe. The only people who could pay a hunter, won't."

Talga's grip on my hand loosened for a moment. Then they clasped it tighter, as if they were just becoming conscious of the touch. "That cone I found. It's a sensor, isn't it?"

"Saying when to drop the doors?" Khoshet sketched a quick, calligraphic command on her notebook's input page, then jerked her head in bitter confirmation. "It's keyed to a Company code."

Talga offered, "She had an Amaranth jacket." A radio tag could easily have hidden underneath the embroidered purple spikes.

The sadness I had swallowed was spreading through my chest, splitting into tight-curled filaments of rage. The Companies didn't want Talga. Just an unplanned kid, born outside a contract. But they had worked so hard to make their own place. They learned the city, they saved up to buy the velokab, they kept it charged. Now Amaranth had killed my client for reasons I didn't understand—it had to be the Company, she didn't know anyone else on this continent. The Company would have murdered Talga, too, by accident. Or not even by accident. As insurance. Talga was the explanation for any judge or hunter who actually came looking.

Khoshet was rummaging in my supply cupboard, fulfilling the need to do something, anything. She found two more teacups and a bowl of apricot candies. I took one, because Talga needed to eat, so it was with the sour-sweet of the coming summer on my tongue that I said, "I'm going to find them. The Company person who did this."

Khoshet laughed in startlement. It was too much, too huge. Talga shook their head. I shifted all my attention into coaxing them to sleep.

THE NEXT DAY I dressed carefully, choosing a veil a
shade heavier than usual, but a filmier tunic. I got to the
teahouse around the time clerks and managers finish their
work days. There was a long counter along one wall, with
sesame pastries and hashish candy under glass, tea from
three different continents, and different sizes of trays for
sharing. It was a pretty display, though most of the profit
would come from vodka.

I looked for the person working. Not the people in
matching aprons behind the counter, but one of the twelve
thousand flowers, like me. Most tourist teahouses have
someone resident. In this case, it was a man with a close-
trimmed beard and a casually unbuttoned shirt who went
by Esarik. His heavy scent was a mix of teak and orange
blossoms.

I asked Esarik to sit with me and play a game of narda.
Narda boards are long and skinny, with peaked triangles
along the sides. The red counters are Sun employees, the
black counters work for the Deep, and you can't clear
a counter and score its points until it earns a Company
share. You can tell who invented this game, and they
weren't a soldier or a judge. But narda is still a staple
of my trade, because it's contemplative enough to let
you watch a crowd, but you can bet on the dice rolls if
you want to. Esarik was happy to play. Of course, I was
tipping him generously for the privilege. Otherwise, he
couldn't have justified letting me share.

I waited a while, through the after-work rush and the
suppertime lull. Esarik took one client upstairs.

This teahouse got a lot of Company workers. That
wasn't a surprise, in one sense; they tend to move in
clumps. But usually the different Companies quarrel. My
attention was caught by a group of people who had shoved
several couches close together. They were mixed in age
and in affiliation. One young man had the fluffy beard
of someone growing it out for the first time, and a green

Cypress hat. A man in gold and black watched the door, soft lamplight half-smoothing the pouches under his eyes. And there was a woman with strong, lined hands and an Amaranth badge on her shoulder, raising her glass in a toast. The others echoed, "Solidarity."

A burly man wearing a shirt with pearly buttons joined the group, shrugging in a dramatic apology. The man who had been watching the door said something, and the burly man turned the side of his head toward him, rolling up the soft edge of the cap over his ear.

I remembered the lilac and green ribbon under the edge of my client's scarf. This was her group, I was certain. I smiled at the burly man, who grinned back with the air of a man who has made a budget and is sticking to it.

The group was arguing about something—how to decide when new members could start wearing its braid, I guessed—but it was too amorphous and unwieldy to make real decisions. That happened in pairs and threes, when people got up to choose pastries together, or waited in line for the toilets, or went outside to get a breath of air. The man with the heavy eyes was still watching the door. He seemed a little disconcerted, but not sad. I wondered who had found my client's body, and who they told.

Eventually the group broke up. The younger crowd went to find a cafe that had water-pipes, and the older crowd went back to their hotel rooms, and ostensibly to bed. The man with the fluffy beard went back to his hotel room, too, and I went with him. There were two people's clothes strewn everywhere, fancy coats and workout gear, but his roommate was off smoking water-pipes. He was energetic and curious: we tried the bed and the shower.

I was halfway dressed again and trying to blot my hair dry when he tugged on my Aid Collective ribbon. "It's shiny. Like a river."

"A mirror for the deep pools of my eyes? It's for the Association of Twelve Thousand Flowers."

He laughed. "Surprise! I know what you do now!"

"Brilliant! Simply brilliant deductions!" I rested my damp head on his shoulder. "But you missed the 'association' part. Any businessperson has bad days. When you're sick, or exhausted. Or if you're much too energetic, and want the fees for an anatomy class. We all chip in, and the Association is there when we need it."

"No, that really is brilliant. You've reinvented collective aid. It's an ancient philosophy, from before the saint's wars—I've got a book somewhere—" He rummaged in the pile beside the bed. I bit my tongue, and didn't list any of the philosophers I have read.

The book, when he unearthed it, was a slim volume, printed on the kind of machine that extrudes its own paper, with stars and underlining from at least three different people. He pressed it on me. I didn't even have to fake my gratitude: it was a manual for forming Aid Collectives. Jade miners from all the Companies were cooperating. No wonder Amaranth was worried.

I was back at the teahouse the next evening, and so was your miners' collective. It was a slightly smaller group this time—the burly man and my friend with the fluffy beard were both absent—and the mood was bitter. They were eating sliced sausages and pickled carrots, and remembering disasters: a cave-in, a hand crushed, an ordinary infection that a medic should have caught. They listed names of friends lost, and for every one there was a toast.

Esarik nudged me and said quietly, "She's drinking water."

He meant the woman I had first seen toasting, the one
with the lined hands and the sharp Amaranth flowers
splashed across her jacket sleeve. There's no shame in
answering a toast with fruit juice or chilled tea. But this
woman was drinking clear liquid in small glasses, just
like all the other collective members. Indeed, she was
organizing the toasts: she fetched tray after tray of them,
in glasses half the colors of the rainbow. She always took
the yellow glass. She probably claimed it was a lucky color.

She noticed me watching the group and smiled, a slow
and measured smile. She had surprisingly lovely lashes,
thick and soft against her weather-roughened face.

When the party broke up, she walked to our table and said,
"I think I have found a friend," in a voice a little too loud.

Esarik said, "Perhaps two friends," meaning that he
would distract her if I wanted a safer client. I smiled, slid
the dice toward him, and thanked him for the game.

The Amaranth woman and I walked out of the
teahouse hand in hand, as if we were not new friends but
old ones reunited. When we were back at street level she
kissed me up against the railing, pushing my tunic up
past my waist. Enthusiasm, maybe, or maybe a test: there
are certain lines a hunter will not cross. I tipped my head
back and kissed her deep.

My tablet chimed, with a notification Khoshet had set
up. It meant that somebody was trying to break in.

I was breathing too fast, but that might look
professional. I ran my hand down my new client's back
and asked if she had a hotel room.

She laughed, "A surety!" and checked her own tablet, in
the casual way of someone wondering about the time.

Mine chimed again, with the notification for, "I am
providing data from a false identity."

She set her arm around my waist and took me to a
hotel. It was the same hotel my friend with the fluffy
beard had frequented, but she was on the thirty-fifth floor,

instead of the tenth. The center of the room was taken up by a vast circular carpet with the hotel's logo, in gold on red.

My new client traced her fingers along the edge of my veil and down my jawline and nibbled on my lips. Her hands were strong, on my face and holding to my shoulder. I would have rested on them and ignored the coming morning, with any other client.

When she hit a switch on the wall, the carpet shivered into slices and curled away, and a bed rose from the center, piled with golden pillows. I parted my lips in admiration, set my lips to her ear, and asked about the contract.

We sank onto the golden bed together, and she gave me her face. My tablet displayed the hash, black and white dull behind the city lights, but I kept a true image, too. I won't tell you about the ribbons braided in her hair. I swore confidentiality, and I keep my promises. But I can tell you that when I lifted the crisp kerchief from her hair, a twist of lilac and green ribbon fell away in my hand.

If you seek justice for your friend in the Collective—if you can believe one of twelve thousand flowers—the agent you're looking for has this face.

THE
LAST TUTOR

in the year 3377 of the Nakhorian reckoning

ISEKENDRIYA ZUHROVA, HEIR to five-eighths of a share in Fountain Company, knew their tutor was already drafting his resignation letter. Thus, they submitted to his inspection with comparative good grace.

"If you take a soft brush to your eyebrows, you can accentuate the curve," the tutor suggested.

Ise cut him off with a jerk of their chin: no makeup.

Their best coat was too big. The tailor had run their measurements through a growth algorithm for fifteen-year-olds before cutting the fabric, and Ise had failed to meet the growth curve's expectations, along with everybody else's.

The embroidered fabric jutted over their bony shoulders like so much folded paper. Their wrists were covered by their undershirt, of near-translucent lawn. It was too fine to hide the bruises and scratches.

"Dare I ask?" said the tutor, which Ise thought was ridiculous, since he was asking.

"I found a boulder on the north estate with a native lichen." Fat plum-colored drops spilling over the edge, like flash-frozen jam.

"You climbed up to look?"

"I investigated the alien lifeform." Ise spoke scornfully but ironically: they were the alien, on Nakharat.

Their tutor, unmoved by cyanobacteria-analogue symbionts, simply sighed. "You didn't have time to rest your wrists in the healing accelerator?"

"I didn't want to disturb Mother."

It was a weak excuse, but it was now unanswerable. Nobody wanted to disturb Ise's mother an hour before a party. "Find a bracelet," said their tutor. "I know you have a good one."

Ise had matching cuffs of carved green jade, hinged and capped with gold. They fetched them and let their tutor clasp them round their wrists, fastening the delicate chain. "There are leaves here like the Saint of Vines," he pointed out.

All of Ise's tutors had this problem. They thought that because Ise was neither a girl nor a boy they would be obsessed with fucking mysticism and want to spend all their time reading poetry about the ineffable oneness of the universe. The Saint of Vines, if they existed, would not love Ise. No one did.

"How much do you think these cuffs are worth?" they asked. "3200 credits each?" They chose the number deliberately: it was their tutor's monthly salary.

"More than that, I expect," said their tutor, tone now chill. "You would have to ask your mother."

Ise's father was already in the receiving room when Ise and their tutor entered. A couple of his colleagues stood by the windows, noses almost pressed against the glass as they gazed along the valley and up the slope, tracing the path where the train tracks ran. The chief engineer from the Amaranth Company outpost just over the pass nodded vigorously at Ise's father; their turban was swirled with Amaranth purple. The tall woman beside them had the flared coat and flickering gaze that suggested Physical Security; Ise assumed the stiff brocade concealed a gun.

Ise favored their father—they had his wide cheekbones and sharply pointed chin—but where he was compact, they were a bundle of wires. They bowed jerkily but correctly, as befitted a Fountain Company heir. "Father. Chief Engineer. Madam. I am pleased to join you with my tutor, Scholar Nawriz Bahev."

"Bahev, you will make the chief comfortable, will you not?" said Ise's father. "Isekendriya, come and meet the others."

Scholar Bahev fell upon the engineer with the air of a man starved for adult conversation, even mining budgets. As Ise's father drew them away, he was already proposing a toast. Ise got to toast too, a real adult toast with vodka in a tiny blue glass. They swallowed their cough and smiled their best company smile.

More of Father's colleagues trickled in, some heading to the windows, some to the buffet. There was one more woman, her veil spangled with Fountain silver in quarter-circles. Mother wasn't going to like that.

Ise's mother waited to make her appearance until the sun sank behind the far hills and the Twin Planets glittered on the horizon. The light by the doorway brightened as she entered. Her coat was the deep blue, almost shading to green, of a half-kilometer-deep mountain lake; her brows arched like the rise and fall of moons. She led Ise's little brother by one delicate hand. Mirek had let her line his eyes with kohl. Ise shoved their tongue against their teeth to keep from hissing.

The woman with the spangled veil spun, pulled toward Mother as marbled paint follows a brush. Ise shouldn't have worried. Another triumph for Mother. And for Mirek, her best prop.

Ise stuck by the window, close to their father and a cluster of his colleagues: the woman from Physical Security, a younger man whose beard had silver patches along his jaw and a black thumbprint beneath his lower lip, another man with a soft felt cap and jutting ears, and Father's favorite rival Assessor Gulnarev, whose curly beard was entirely white.

"We saw so many animals from the train," said Physical Security. "Antelope, elk...I hope the hunting here in your mountains is as good, Amirhanov!"

Father laughed. "Tell me tomorrow evening if you're satisfied!"

"We had lots of time to choose our ideal targets," said Big Ears. "The train dawdled along."

Right through an antelope migration path, not that he gave a fuck.

Black Thumbprint nodded vigorously at his friend. "I've never understood the lack of a real high-speed train. This continent is small. You should be able to board after your first cup of tea in Tengiz-Ushiyet and disembark the next morning by the eastern ocean."

"Do you want to be on a train going three hundred kilometers an hour when it hits an elk?" asked Physical Security.

Black Thumbprint shrugged. "I'd be fine. I wouldn't want to be the elk."

"The real danger is another train," observed Gulnarev.

"Or a switching problem," said Ise's father. "Kostyanov, you and Kamilev may be too young to remember this, but about twenty years ago, the Fishercats reprogrammed a switch. A fifty-car train was halfway across when it flipped, and the whole length jackknifed."

Thumbprint whistled. "Fucking gearfishers. How many people died?"

"It was a freight train, but I believe it had a conductor, so...one? Millions of credits lost, though."

But it wasn't only one person. It was one person that the adults cared about: they were skilled at overlooking everyone else. "One conductor plus one engine," Ise insisted.

"Yes, Ise," said their father, solemnly. "What's more, we are fortunate there was no chemical spill. The Fishercats preach that the planet is a garden, but when it comes to specific lives, they are careless."

"They're used to careening around the steppe in hopped-up go-carts," said Big Ears. (That must be Kamilev. Eight hells, Ise hoped Mother wasn't planning to quiz them on the names.)

Thumbprint—Kostyanov—expanded on the theme: "Then they come to the cities and get pissed when we complain about petty theft. Fuck gardening! The gearfishers wish we'd go away and leave our toys behind."

On second thought, Ise didn't *want* to know their names.

Physical Security frowned, assessing Father's stature, his sparse and close-trimmed beard. "There are plenty of Fishercats in the cities. Failed business owners, lawsuit losers, disaffected students."

"Half those students thought they'd be judges themselves, till they failed their exams," said Gulnarev.

Ise wondered if their tutor had planned to be a judge, instead of a teacher. They should mention gavels and see if he twitched.

Big Ears was chewing on his lip. "About that jackknifed train. What I don't understand is, why didn't the engine *slow*? The train should have started decelerating the moment it realized something was wrong with that switch."

His friend Thumbprint gripped his shoulder and shook, laughing. "That's the whole point of the operation, asshole. The gearfishers hacked the switch and spoofed its check-ins. The engine didn't know."

"And that," said Physical Security, "is why lattice security matters just as much as my work."

"That sounds like a toast!" Gulnarev declared. "Shall we toast to that, Zuhr Amirhanov? The security of Fountain Company?"

Ise's father filled everyone's glasses, and they knocked the shots back. Vodka wasn't so different from mountain water, Ise thought, if mountain water burned.

Near the buffet, Ise's tutor fumbled and dropped a skewer. He covered for it by proposing a toast with the Amaranth engineer, whose cheeks were beginning to flush.

Ise's father's friends were arguing about train routes now. "If the north is too cold, why not try the south?" suggested Big Ears. "Run a spur over a pass and pick up traffic from some of the coastal towns."

Thumbprint nodded vigorously. "It's stupid not to have an alternative to crossing the steppe. All that emptiness means you don't know where you'll find a suicide bomber. Or a suicidal antelope."

He was blaming the wildlife for Fountain Company's bad design. At least the southern line was missing for a reason. Ise protested, "It's not that nobody has thought about building new tracks, it's that the whole base of the south coast mountains is a swamp. You have to think about how the water falls and where it spreads, or your freight will sink into the muck."

The Amaranth engineer drifted closer, drawn by the talk of rocks and water. "I worked for an operation outside Zhasau for a few years. We were always pumping."

"Zhasau is all marsh," agreed Ise. "Lots of bitterns, though."

"Isekendriya," said their tutor, following his friend,

"I thought you hated geography."

"Oh, no!" said Physical Security cheerfully. "Ise is Amirhanov's child. They've been telling us all about where to build the next Fountain line. Ise, if you had to run tracks south, which pass would you choose to go toward the sea?"

"Don't be shy!" Gulnarev was beaming. Ise would bet their bracelets he had seen their tutor's glare.

"Applied geography is different," Ise said weakly. It was no good; their father and their tutor were both listening, and one of the two men wouldn't like what they heard.

Choosing whom to fail was not so hard. Ise braced their shoulders. "So...your options for a pass are Usik and Yellowhead. Usik Pass is higher, but there's a ridge running towards it that will lift you out of the swamp. And it leads to Savda, which is 50% larger than Duckport, where Yellowhead would take you. I'd use Usik."

"Ise," said their tutor, "you told me you didn't know the difference between Savda and Tengiz-Ushiyet."

"It's eighteen hundred kilometers and three climate zones," said Ise. "I remember the essay."

"I remember the essay, too. I read every little word of it. When did you write it?"

Ise's gaze flickered. Know your space and know your enemies. There were seven people within earshot. The closest was their father. He could easily cuff their ears, but he wouldn't do that now. Mother was still talking to the woman with the quarter-moon veil.

Ise took a deep breath and projected. They didn't want to have to say this twice. "I wrote the essay contrasting Savda and Tengiz-Ushiyet when I was ten."

"*When I was ten.*" Ise's tutor imitated their voice in a high-pitched whine. It was fucking insulting: they weren't even a high tenor. "You recopied your infant work in new calligraphy and made me suffer through it? Green saint, what *else* did you lie about, Isekendriya? Have you ever had a thought that wasn't stolen?"

He was making them sound like Mirek. Ise bowed so that he wouldn't see their face. "I regret my insufficiencies, Scholar Bahev."

"I regret my presence on this side of the continent." Scholar Bahev gathered his flowing coats and stormed out. The effect was spoiled when he tripped over a low table near the door.

Father frowned impartially and Physical Security's eyes kept moving, but Thumbprint and the Amaranth engineer were frankly staring. It was a scene. Ise had created a scene. The knowledge settled over them like a lead-weighted net.

They checked the cluster where their mother stood, hoping she was absorbed in conversation—they were struggling against their failure, the way a bird would struggle. But Ise's mother was turning away from them, raising a fluted glass in yet another toast.

Knots and wires. That meant she had been watching all along.

ISE WATCHED THEIR tutor leave on the house cameras, and stayed awake until his resignation letter pinged their tablet. They would have a morning of freedom before the storm. They set their alarm to start playing finch and sparrow calls before dawn.

Father and his friends would hunt along the valleys. Ise chose an antelope trail that went more or less straight up. They hoped to glimpse a real fisher cat or one of the smaller tawny-throated martens. Some small part of them, the part that had listened to too many of their nurse's tales, felt they ought to apologize to the beasts for

Thumbprint's rudeness. There was nothing wrong with being clever about gears. There was nothing *wrong* with caring about the trains.

But Ise saw no fisher cats, and no antelope either: nothing bigger than the plump and bobbing ground squirrels. They found a stream they knew. It had more rocks than water, in this part of the summer, but they followed it upward, balancing on the boulders and watching the dragonflies flicker and zag around them.

They perched on a flat rock to eat their lunch. Their house and the other estate buildings were hidden by the curve of the mountain. Instead Ise looked out, to the sweep of the hills rising across the valley. Cedar and pine; higher up there would be rhododendrons and lupine. The peaks in the distance were crinkled. Indigenous lichen might hold on, there. Lichen and ice.

Ise heard a plop from the water below them and bent slowly, trying to peer into the water without casting a strange shadow. Their patience was rewarded by an orange streak and a wet glinting that resolved, as their eyes adjusted, into the figure of a Vraselian salamander. It was swimming toward the center of the pool, its six legs resting as its powerful tail beat back and forth. Vraselian salamanders were tough. They bore live tadpoles and ate everything from crickets to young trout. They had been one of the first vertebrates introduced to Nakharat. Ise liked them.

Ise turned up rocks beside the stream until they had a collection of millipedes. They deposited their collection in a divot of earth beside the pool, along with one live slug, and settled in to wait. The salamander approached cautiously, swimming by from one direction, then the other. At last it scuttled straight up, moving sideways—the extra legs helped it flip from one vector to another—and knocked the slug into the pool.

"To the destruction of our enemies!" Ise told it, sipping from their water bottle in a tiny toast.

What would the salamander say if it could answer? Would it toast to the preservation of its friends?

Bright stars, Ise wished they had a friend. They would bring them millipedes every single day.

Ise straggled back down the mountainside in the late afternoon. As their tablet came into range of the house node, it chimed three times: first with a notice their mother had scheduled a meeting for ten in the morning, then with the sad tone of a missed meeting, and finally with a note she had rescheduled for tomorrow. "If a conversation with your parent will not disturb your active schedule."

Well, it wasn't like Ise could be *more* fucked.

There would be a less formal reception that evening, after the hunters returned, so Ise showered and dressed in their second-best coat, the one with the hand-knotted buttons. They still had a bit of time, and they had no tutor to assess their preparations, so they slipped into the north wing of the house and went to find their old nurse.

Ise's nurse was short and round, though not as short as Ise. She had the broad nose and rolling hips of the steppe rovers, those descendants of early planet-gardeners who roamed the continent assessing what they had wrought. She also had bad knees. They puffed and swelled, not from the erosion of increased age, but because her body fought itself. The conventional medicines were mostly poison: they besieged the body until it counterattacked, rather than tearing its own joints apart. The healing accelerator was gentler and safer. But it needed power and regular maintenance. It wasn't the sort of thing you could pack into a caravan.

Besides, she loved Mirek. She even—unaccountably, amazingly—loved Ise.

"Let me brush your hair," she told Ise now.

Ise was nearly old enough for an adult turban. They could braid their own hair. But it was wonderful to sit on a low stool and feel the regular pressure of the brush.

Sometimes their nurse patted their shoulder out of sheer companionship, and Ise had to fight not to purr like a cat.

Their nurse used a hair oil with a sharp green scent, like crushed perilla leaves. "You're getting big, Iselika. Soon you'll need more ribbons than just Fountain blue."

Ise blushed all over. Even their shoulders felt hot. Where the fuck did she imagine they were going to find a girlfriend? On the side of a mountain? "I would have to—"

"They would have to stop looking like the back half of a stick insect," Mirek said, coming back from the kitchens. He had a sesame bun in one hand and a toy train in the other. It was painted with huge round eyes, the lashes nearly as long as his.

"Mirhanek! Show your sibling some respect."

Mirek stuffed half the bun in his mouth and bowed, mumbling.

Ise scrambled to their feet. "Thank you for brushing my hair."

"Ise's running away 'cause they're in trouble," Mirek said, in a confidential whisper that wasn't soft at all.

"I'm not! Father likes me to be timely."

"They missed a meeting with Mother, and now they're going to cry. But it's not their fault." Mirek was addressing his toy train now, holding it out and gazing into its fake eyes. "Ise can't help it if nobody likes them. Everyone simply likes us better."

"Mirek!"

"Yes, honored sibling?" Mirek glanced sideways at Ise, eyelids fluttering, then gave his train a wet and smacking kiss.

"Mirek," Ise said. Their vision narrowed in rage. They could see nothing except his horrible wet grin. "Mirek, has anyone ever told you why your trains have a face?"

"Because they're adorable like I am?"

"Because there are people bound inside them, with wires threaded through their brains. Trains have to choose, sometimes, which track to follow. If they make the wrong choice, somebody might die. But it's not fair to leave a life-or-death decision to something without a soul. So we take souls. We trap people inside the engines, and we drug them, and we never, ever let them out."

"People like me?" Mirek's wide-eyed expression was one Ise had never seen before. It looked like fear.

"Could be. You're a hardened criminal."

"Isekendriya—"

Whatever their nurse meant to say was drowned by Mirek's screaming. Ise bowed and fled.

The beginning of the reception was easy. Ise had no tutor to monitor, or vice versa. The woman with the spangled veil had killed an elk. She was proud of it, glorying in her unexpected facility with a rifle. She even tolerated Gulnarev's attempts to give advice. Ise asked which rifle everyone had used, and didn't laugh at Big Ears whining for a shotgun.

Mirek appeared before Mother this time. He ignored Ise in favor of starfruit and peaches. Ise turned their back to him and interviewed Physical Security about her favorite handgun. Semi-automatic Pellona Eight, was the answer. Tough, and perhaps too big for Ise's hands. They longed to admire it, but handguns and toasting didn't mix.

Mother was wearing white tonight. Her coat was sewn of thousands of silk lozenges, stitched with silver thread so they rippled like a stream as she moved. Everyone turned; even Physical Security's eyes were trapped.

And Mirek, darling Mirek, chose that moment to inquire, "Mother, is it true they're going to stab a needle through my brainstem and lock me in the dark?"

"Amirhanek, sweetling. Who told you that?"

"Ise says, the trains—" He mewed as if he was swallowing a sob. One fat tear trembled from his lashes.

Ise had seen this trick before. It involved hanging your head shyly and a glass of ice water. "The trains are for bad people, Mirek."

"The trains are for people who were raised wrong. The judges who look after everyone know that some people need a quiet space to learn better. They're studying how to take responsibility in a controlled environment." Mother bent and hugged Mirek, every motion as graceful as a handmade waterfall.

Mirek gazed over her shoulder at Ise, smiling what must have looked, to other people, like a tremulous smile.

ISE SPENT THE next morning practicing the names of all their father's guests. They made a little game, using camera footage from the house systems and the list Mother had given to the head of staff, and drilled forwards and backwards until they could not even confuse Kostyanov and Kamilev. Mother would extract from them a catalog of faults; there was no reason to hand her new ones.

They presented themself at the door of her office at ten o'clock exactly. The house system opened the door for them. They heard it lock behind them.

Mother's office was all glass and blue gauze. The only window was a skylight; all the rest was vinelike lamps and mirrors. Ise was too old to disrobe for punishment, so they simply bowed and waited.

"By the round table," said their mother. "I moved the vase."

The table was made of thick, earthquake-proof glass, supported by a silver metal cage. Ise rested their hands upon it, palms up. The scratches on their wrists had not yet faded. Mother rotated them, her hands hovering a few centimeters from their shoulders, until they were facing a narrow mirror.

Ise gazed forward. A small person, in a black shirt, with two braids. They could be anyone's child, or nobody's at all. Certainly their mother, with a face like smooth marble and crystals dangling from her ears, was from another realm entirely.

"Review for me, Zuhrova, your failures of the day before yesterday."

Mother was naming them as their father's child. That was very bad. "I irritated my tutor, and did not observe his behavior at the party, so he got drunk. Then I bragged to Father's friends about geography, and my tutor called me a liar."

"Are you a liar, Zuhrova?"

Eyes straight ahead. Mirror like still water. "I tricked my tutor into asking for an essay on a subject that I studied years ago."

"Why did you do that?"

Because I couldn't bear to read another poem about the inevitability of justice. "Because I am lazy."

Ise's mother moved to face them, blocking the mirror. She was holding the rod she used to adjust her many drapes. It was inlaid with spirals made of shell. "Will you pay the price for your faults, Zuhrova?"

Ise maintained eye contact, focusing on their breathing. Out then in. It was better to remain relaxed. "I will pay."

The rod fell across their right palm. Its end cracked on the earthquake-proof glass. Standing. Ise had to keep standing, through the pain. Nothing shattered.

"Very well." Light fingertips, fluttering over the aching mark. "Summarize yesterday's failures."

Mother wasn't going to meet with Mirek. She never

met with Mirek. Ise was the eldest, and the responsibility
was theirs. "I was angry at my brother for saying I looked
like a stick insect, so I told him about the people bound
into the trains. He asked me about them after the hunt."

"Why did he do that?"

Mirek set Ise up because he liked to win. That was the
only reason anyone in this family did anything. "He said
he was scared."

"What was the result?"

Fuck, what answer did she want? What was the worst
effect, of all of Ise's compounded failures? "I embarrassed
the household."

"You need a stronger verb."

Mother sounded kind. Only force of will kept Ise from
crawling under her desk, like they had when they were
five. "I entangled the household? With some scheme of
Father's colleagues?"

Mother only waited, her mouth curving in an expression
of deep sorrow.

Wires of Hell. "I endangered the household."

Mother nodded slowly.

"I made it appear that there might be a person within
the household who had Fishercat sympathies. Who
was telling me and Mirek stories." Fuck, fuck, fuck. Ise
deserved everything Mother was about to do to them.

"And is there such a person, Isekendriya?" Oh, the
benevolence Mother could project, when she knew she
had won.

"No, Mother. I was selfish and reckless, all by myself."

Mother slammed Ise's left hand with the rod, like she was
closing a book she hated. Ise squeaked. They would have
hated themself for the sound, but they were too focused on
the star of pain in their palm. It was the brightest thing they
had ever felt. Brighter even than the jewels in Mother's veil.

"You may go, Ise."

Ise blinked as hard as they could. They weren't sure if they could move yet. "Mother, forgive me. I think you just broke my hand."

"Don't overdramatize, darling."

Mother lifted Ise's hand in hers. Ise bit their tongue until they tasted blood. They needed to move the pain to something they were in charge of.

Eight hells, they couldn't stand it. One tear fell.

"I suppose you'll have to put it through the healing accelerator. How tiresome."

The accelerator lived in Mother's office, behind a drape covered in trumpetflowers. Ise sat in the chair that Mother placed and shivered at the first injection. The pain hid itself behind a curtain. Manageable.

Mother set her own chair and took Ise's other hand. "Isekendriya, I am worried that you don't have a consistent mentor."

"I have books and the lattice." And Nurse.

"I know that you and your brother respect your old nurse very much"—where had Mother learned to read minds?—"but her concerns are parochial. Fountain Company is global, Isekendriya. You will need to deal with people and problems from every continent."

With Mother, things always came back to West Continent— the place with the space elevators, and fashion, and Fountain Company headquarters. She didn't care about the mountains. There was a reason her windows only showed the sky.

"I should not have driven away my tutors," Ise said. They spoke formulaically, because the healing accelerator was starting to work, and they could feel the weird achey glow of bone growing.

Mother petted their right hand with her slender fingers. "Promise me you will not lie to your next tutor."

If Ise could have broken free, they would have, but the accelerator's threads were inside their skin and there was nowhere for them to go. "I promise."

"Your word, Ise."

"I give my word, as an heir to Fountain Company, that I will not lie to my next tutor."

"Good child.—But you're almost all grown up, aren't you? Even Mirek is getting bigger. I think, if your next tutor leaves before the year is out, I will send your nurse away as well. You shouldn't be repining over childish things."

But Nurse needed the accelerator. She needed the thing that was mending Ise's bones with coals and calcium thread. "Don't worry, Mother. I will study very hard."

Mother interlaced her fingers with Ise's in a parody of a braid. "Excellent. The house will tell me when you're done here; I suppose I'll leave you to it. If you take a wrist brace, you may say it is for repetitive stress. You spend too much time messing with the lattice."

"Thank you, Mother." Ise tried to match her sweetness, but they had to drag the words through their body, ignoring the fire in their hands.

They watched their mother leave through the mirrors. Her reflection flowed across the room, veil swaying in gentle and inexorable waves, like Ise's pain.

THE NEW TUTOR was a woman. She had a high forehead and long earlobes and fingernails painted copper, and she was the second-most-beautiful person Ise had ever met. Her name was Scholar Tohmishevet.

Scholar Tohmishevet had sewn a button back onto her coat with the wrong color thread. It was a fortuitous sloppiness: if she had not been so tall and so shabbily dressed, Ise's mother would have sent her straight back to the station by the quickest route that avoided Ise's father.

Instead, Scholar Tohmishevet unpacked her bag of clothes and her case of books and went to bed early.

The next morning, she invited Ise to tea. It was a very adult sort of tea meeting, with candied hazelnuts that Scholar Tohmishevet had brought on the train and eggs molded into star patterns. She offered Ise a choice of red or black tea. Ise chose black, with extra jam.

Ise exerted themself to make adult conversation. They learned that Scholar Tohmishevet had never been a tutor before (though she had assisted for university courses), that she did not like to hunt, and that the weather on her departure had been fair. She had previously shared a flat with two roommates, and one of those roommates had owned a cat.

This was the point in the conversation where ordinarily Ise would say something awful. They would ask whether Tohmishevet had been dumped by her lover, or why her political economy scores were so low, or what the fuck was going on with that mismatched thread. It was easiest when tutors hated Ise early. It saved a lot of stomach-curling disappointment.

But Ise wasn't allowed to drive this tutor off. Worse, they found they didn't want to. She smiled a little bit too wide when she chose her next egg, revealing a chipped tooth that the healing accelerator could fix in five minutes. Ise wished they could be friends with her. They could walk with her, hand in hand beside a wide river.

Knots and stars, it was going to hurt when Ise fucked this up.

They tried a couple of other conversation topics, fruitlessly, and asked at last, "Aren't you going to give me some sort of test?"

"You have scored between the 85th and 88th percentile on every standardized exam you have been given for the last three years. It is remarkable precision. I don't think I will learn anything new."

The exams were always administered by the house lattice, and Ise had lived in this house all their life. It would be embarrassing if they couldn't get the scores they wanted. 87th percentile was perfect: neither good enough to tempt extra assignments, nor bad enough to merit a report to their parents. "I suppose you know what to do with me, then."

"I am not sure I do know, Isekendriya. What would you like to learn?"

Ise shrugged helplessly. "Linear algebra?" When in doubt, pick a subject the lattice was good at.

Scholar Tohmishevet took yet another egg, smearing its yolk across a wedge of toast. "What do you do when you're not studying?"

Ise would have told any other tutor that they liked lattice games, and generated trivia about planetbuilder strategy until the tutor kicked them out in disgust. But they had given their word not to lie, and they were worried Scholar Tohmishevet would get egg yolk stuck under her beautiful copper fingernails, and before they knew it they were admitting, "I go outside. I explore up the mountain."

"What have you found?"

"Frogs and salamanders, mostly. Some Nakharat lichens." Conjoined stars, they were blushing. Their nose was getting red. If Mirek saw them like this, they would die.

Scholar Tohmishevet sipped her tea, which let Ise look down and recover. "Have you ever conducted a formal ecological study?"

"I can do that?"

"Why shouldn't you? Citizen science is important."

Fuck, they had almost contradicted her. "I regret the appearance of surprise, Scholar Tohmishevet. My other tutors were poets."

She laughed, making no attempt to hide the chipped tooth. "I suppose that tells me who's job-hunting. In all seriousness, Isekendriya, we will have to send out for the appropriate test tubes and filters—I assume you have streams somewhere, for your frogs to swim in?—but then you can gather data on water quality and bacteria ratios at least until the snow falls. Maybe longer, if you've got the right gear."

Ise stared. Their tutor was telling them to wander around the mountains? For educational benefit? There had to be a catch.

There was a catch, the same one that there always was. "Mother doesn't like it when I go exploring. She thinks I'm too much like my grandfather." Like Father's father, who had walked off the steppe, chosen a name meaning "ruler of rulers," and refactored Fountain Company security for half the continent. Grandfather Amirhan won his half-share through his own hard work. But Mother didn't approve of steppe rover methods. Never ask whom her own grandmother had been.

"I see. Then we will tell your parents you are engaged in an applied statistics project, and I will teach you enough statistics to make it utter truth. Have we a deal?"

"We do." Ise would offer a ribbon for it, but they were too young for formal contracts. They said, instead, "Please, call me Ise."

"And you may call me Tamyet." That same glorious, unconstrained smile. Ise wished they knew what the fuck she *wanted*.

Ise knew what was happening to them. They had researched the processes of puberty extensively, when they were deciding what should happen to their body. (Their body had its own ideas about height.) They knew they were prone to intense admirations at this age, that it was a necessary process of ego-development that would create a stable matrix for adult relationships, and that their feelings would eventually moderate to a refined nostalgia productive of great poetry.

That wasn't why they began spying on their tutor. They began spying on their tutor because she had given them something they wanted desperately, and at some point they were going to have to pay for it, and they had no way in all the hells and all the spheres above to estimate its price.

They started with the report from the tutoring agency, and the more detailed though less accessible report from Father's staff. Scholar Tohmishevet had been born in Savda and had attended university on the plains; her specialty was the philosophy of engineering; she had no consistent lovers. She was fond of gambling, though not so fond as to constitute an addiction, her closest living relative was a brother who worked in the Gentian Company mines, and she collected images of tropical fish. There were no strong connections to other Companies, no unexplained influxes or outlays of credits; Father's staff rated the probability of corporate espionage as very low.

Ise wondered, though, about their tutor's missing parent. Much of their wonder was envy. It would be so wonderful, to be without a family—it must feel like stepping off the mountainside and flying. But they knew other people had warmer feelings about *their* families, and as Father was fond of saying, every significant security breach started with a feeling.

Ise couldn't ask their tutor directly. They had no way to frame the sentences. But Mirek had no qualms and Ise had no reason not to lie to him, so they took the first opportunity of asking, "Did you know that Scholar Tohmishevet's parent died from eating starfruit?"

Mirek regarded them with suspicion. "Which parent?"

"She only had one. They were an accountant. They were so allergic that they puffed up like a porcupine and burst."

"Why did they eat it, then?"

"They only tried it once. It was so juicy they couldn't help themself."

"I don't believe you. I'm going to ask Mother."

Ise shook their head, braids bouncing. "Mother doesn't care about other people's parents. You'd have to ask Tamyet."

Mirek scrunched his nose up when he heard the nickname. He couldn't bear for Ise to be on good terms with someone before he was.

Ise spent the next few days going up the mountain and down the mountain. They had satellite maps of the streams they knew, but those were drawn from photos that flattened elevation. Ise had to calibrate an altimeter, and test it, and mark the height of every tiny pool. They saw many frogs, three antelope, a multitude of birds, and one more Vraselian salamander; they heard the rippling call of a hawk owl. In the evenings they tested rock-slime for cyanobacteria analogues and read papers by other citizen scientists. They were all written by teams of people, school classes or municipal clubs; nobody else worked alone like Ise.

At night, after most of the adults had gone to bed, they reviewed the house's camera footage. They were soon rewarded by an image of Mirek gazing up at their tutor, his eyes impossibly wide.

Extracting the audio was harder. The house usually reserved that data for Ise's parents, but Ise reminded it that their tutor was technically subject to the head of staff and fed in his codes. At last they heard Mirek saying, "Scholar Tohmishevet, I'm so sorry about your parent."

"Thank you, Mirhanek," said their tutor, startled. "It was a long time ago."

"Is it true that—" Mirek's whisper was too high and soft for the house microphones to resolve, but Ise could guess that it involved the words "starfruit" and "burst".

Scholar Tohmishevet's face wobbled as her lips twitched in a circle. When she made it still again, she said, "Not quite. My parent had an unexpected allergy to a medication."

"That's awful! Were they very sick? Were you scared?"

Tohmishevet spoke with the serenity of someone who has trained all her life to lift a boulder. "At first I was very scared. But all the judges and all the Companies came together, and they made it so no one would die of an allergy like that ever again."

"I will eat an entire starfruit in their honor," Mirek told her.

The audio cut out in the middle of her laugh.

The next afternoon, over tea, Scholar Tohmishevet asked Ise, "Did you, by chance, tell your brother that my parent died from an allergic reaction?"

Fucking uncontrollable red flush. "Yes."

"May I ask where you learned that information?"

"There was a report to Father, and I wanted—" Bright stars, this was as bad as putting their hand inside the healing accelerator. "I wanted to know more about you."

"But it only specified an allergic reaction? Not what sort?"

"Yes, Scholar Tohmishevet." Voice small. Eyes raised. Ise shouldn't think about the log-spiral of her earlobes.

They needed to relax, in case she hit them.

Their tutor's voice eased a fraction. "Ise, I will tell you this because you are my friend, but I would ask you not to share it. The reaction is very rare, and nowadays even rarer, because every machine tests for it. But my parent died of an allergy to tacrolimid."

"Like in healing accelerators?" Ise felt like they were scrambling up a slope that wouldn't hold them. The accelerator injected threads of cells that the body could repurpose for new growth. Tacrolimid kept it from rejecting the threads.

"Some people become frightened. They think a healing accelerator might hurt them."

"I'm tougher than I look," Ise said, stoutly.

They wished they had a crystal sword, as in the ancient tales, for their tutor smiled her true wide smile and said, "Somehow, I think you are."

ISE HAD LEARNED that Scholar Tohmishevet was sad. But that was not analysis, it was only data. It was not even very useful data, since the universe was awful more or less uniformly, even if not everyone had noticed. Ise kept looking at the camera footage in the nighttime, hunting for something they couldn't identify, in the same absorbed yet idle way they listened for birdsong or chewed the ends of their braids.

Observing Scholar Tohmishevet was harder than it ought to be. The house system built a model of everyone inside it, learning their probable locations and stray details of their gait. But it was not infallible—it was nowhere near intelligent enough to require a human conscience—and sometimes a household member had valid reasons to access the house system from two places at once. Scholar Tohmishevet had fewer path habits than most people. She met Ise for tea, and she spent long hours in her study, but she rarely socialized with the other household staff members, and she rarely visited the same sequence of rooms in the same order. That inconsistency made the house lose track of her. Ise often saw her arguing with the house system, providing one personal code after another in an effort at authentication, where Nurse or the head of staff or even another tutor would simply have been recognized.

Meanwhile, Ise flipped through images of room after room, hunting Tohmishevet by sight, since the house's trail was broken. One evening they caught Tohmishevet in the corridor outside their mother's office. She used one graceful hand to draw her veil over her shoulder. Her nails were midnight blue.

Ise stuck, like music on a player carried out of data range. Their right hand had already started the flick to the next room. Their whole left arm was ice and bits of lead. She was going to hit them, she was going to hit them and they didn't know, they didn't even know how they had failed—

Bite their tongue. Restart. That wasn't Mother, that was Scholar Tohmishevet.

Eight hells, no. *There are no accidents, there are only careless people.* The confusion existed for a reason.

The confusion existed because Scholar Tohmishevet wanted the house to mix her up with Mother.

Ise should have gone immediately to their father. But Father was away on one of his interminable business trips, and Mother's threat had no loopholes for bad behavior: if Scholar Tohmishevet left on one train, Nurse would leave on the next, no matter how justified this tutor's dismissal had been.

This was all justification for a more fundamental fact: Ise wanted to know. They wanted to know what was going on, and they wanted to find out for themself, and if Mother or Father got hurt while Ise was hunting, that was no more than either of them deserved. If Scholar Tohmishevet got hurt? *Fuck* Scholar Tohmishevet. Fuck her for lying, and pretending to care about Ise, and being stupid enough to get herself caught.

The next afternoon, when Ise shared their latest measurements of conductivity and sulfates with their tutor, they attached to the file an invitation to collaborate. Scholar Tohmishevet, brilliant Tohmishevet, who had won a first in philosophy and published on the long-term stability of cortical array signals and nearly suborned the house—she twisted her stylus and pressed the point down, making the dot for "Yes."

Ise now had access to all the files Scholar Tohmishevet had shared within the house. Most of these were files Tohmishevet shared with Ise. There was a small folder of carnivorous fish videos for Mirek and a folder shared with both of Ise's parents that contained lofty learning goals. "Isekendriya will plan and execute a complex project"— Ise was executing a multilateral surveillance project, monitoring a target even Father had missed. Fountain Company should make them a vice-preceptor.

But the important folder was shared between Mother and Tohmishevet. It held one image of Ise sipping tea and a set of worked problems on p-values. The history was far busier. Ise saw the names of files that originated as Pellona and were tagged as Fountain property. Manuals or mandated procedures, perhaps—they had that kind of dry alphanumeric labeling. But Tohmishevet was transferring them out of the folder into her own locked filespace as quickly as she pulled them in. Ise made a little beetle of a program, something that would hide and carry copies from this folder to their own workspace. Then they settled in to wait.

The sun rose later and later, the ground squirrels grew as fat as scrub acorns, and every afternoon when Ise returned from the mountain they found another file. Tohmishevet was collecting manuals for healing accelerators. Fountain Company didn't manufacture the accelerators, but it owned many and had installed more. Tohmishevet found the names of parts, the recommendations for scheduled maintenance, the ways healing accelerators could be disassembled and transported. Here and there she stored a case study or a failure analysis. Ise looked for tacrolimid, but it only showed up in longer lists of med collections to stock: if Tohmishevet was worried about allergies like her parent's, she was going about it the long way.

Ise still didn't understand. Tohmishevet could have chosen to spy on Pellona Company, or gotten a job at a hospice. Why pose as Ise's tutor? Ise made multiple attempts to worm into Tohmishevet's private files, but those were locked down tight. Besides, she was probably too smart to keep a diary of crimes.

One day the wind blew blustery and cold. Ise filled their test tubes quickly. While they were trudging down the mountainside they were struck by realization, like another gust of wind. There was an entire realm of information about Tohmishevet they had access to, but

had not used. Ise had been ignoring the option because
some childish part of them still thought Tohmishevet was
their friend, and because they wanted to believe they were
a decent person. But neither of these things was true.

Ise wanted to curl up like a millipede when they thought
about their plan. They couldn't sit still. They fidgeted
through all the house and found themself at last in the
north wing. Mirek was wrapped up in a lattice game—Ise
could hear the shrieking of the flutes—so they picked their
way over his half-assembled train tracks to where Nurse sat.

Ise could hardly ask Nurse why they felt like a
salamander snack. Especially when they deserved it. They
flailed and landed on the question, "Why does Mother
never hunt with Father and his friends?"

Nurse looked long and hard at Ise, and just when
they thought she was going to intuit their plan, she said,
"Sometimes two people want the status of a permanent
marriage, but do not have the temperament for it."

Ise felt, suddenly, what it would be like if the house
folded in. If it was a fortress and a boundary, rather than
a gateway to the peaks. Father had excuses to travel,
because of his work; Mother did not.

They couldn't stand it. "I am not bound to have
sympathy for Mother!"

"No," Nurse told them sadly. "No, Iselika, you are not."

In the language of their babyhood, the steppe language
where one could frame an apology without counting
witnesses or cutting lengths of ribbon or naming the true
source of one's regret, Ise said, "I am sorry."

In the same language, Nurse said, "Go to sleep."

But of course Ise didn't go to bed. They went back to
their room, unfolded the threefold screen on their desk,
and double-checked that they had locked the doors. They
got a glass of water, because their mouth tasted like stale
tea gone to mold. Then they asked the house to show
them Scholar Tohmishevet taking off her veil.

Tohmishevet favored long, lightweight scarves—
scarves like Mother's—but her undercap was cheap gray
synthetic. She kept strands from escaping the cap with
snap-clips. Her hair was finer than Ise's.

Ise was an ash vulture. They shouldn't be doing this.
Nobody should see all of a grown person's braids—nobody
but a spouse or a lover or the poets who guided souls to the
long paths of the dead, and that last option was fucking
mythological. That didn't stop Ise from looking.

They saw a white mourning spiral—the black part of
the twist, almost hidden in Tohmishevet's hair, would
be for the hard and secret parts of grief—and the blue
ribbon with white center that belonged to any Fountain
Company employee. The flame-orange ribbon must be
for Tohmishevet's brother: Ise had seen enough pictures of
him on the lattice to recognize his favorite color. The last
ribbon was almost entirely hidden in Tohmishevet's hair.
It shone like oiled steel.

Steel for the Fishercats. Ise was certain of it: gunmetal
gray for the people who loved gears, who broke and built
anew, who cut the train and shipping lines that wove the
world together. Which meant they knew what, but they
were hovering, hovering, and they still didn't know why.

They'd missed something in the accelerator manuals.
They should look again. Ise sorted by authors (often
missing) and by title (full of duplicates). They sorted by file
size out of sheer stubbornness, and saint of fucking vines,
those weren't duplicates after all. Eight files with the same
title and different sizes.

Ise made their tablet compare each pair of manuals,
but the difference was so stark, they could have worked
it out by eye. Each longer manual had an extra section
or chapter, and every one of those chapters was about
extended healing suspension. Extended suspension created
extra maintenance requirements: the accelerator had
to provide the patient with food and oxygen as well as

supporting their healing and managing their waste. You couldn't remove the patient for maintenance: everything had to happen while they were in the tank.

Removing a patient for any reason seemed complex. The guidelines on how to do so were sparse, but the process seemed to involve transfer to a secondary healing accelerator, which could support the autonomic nervous system as the patient slowly woke up.

Ise stopped seeing the manual in front of them, here. All they could hear was a chill voice in their mind repeating "autonomic nervous system" and their own whisper. They were quiet, so quiet. They couldn't risk disturbing the household.

Every star was a knot in Hell, and every knot bound Ise. Extended suspension wasn't for healing. It was for trapping prisoners in the trains.

Ise heard another voice in their memory now: Scholar Tohmishevet telling Mirek, "But all the judges and all the Companies came together..." Why had judges cared about her parent's death? Why hadn't she said "scientists" or "scholars"?

There was a fucking obvious reason, wasn't there?

Tohmishevet's parent would have been called Tohmish. A judge must have sentenced Tohmish for some crime— sentenced them to extended suspension, their body caught in the heart of an engine, their conscience subjugated to the single question of when to stop the train and when to go. The same fate as all the captured Fishercats.

Except it hadn't worked that way. The drug that was supposed to prepare Tohmish for filaments piercing their body and their brain had killed them instead.

There was no point in looking for records of Tohmish's arrest or conviction: Father's team would have found all that data, if it had been unsealed. But the fatal tacrolimid reaction, if it had really happened, should have happened right away.

Ise didn't need the judicial records. They could check the trains. If Tohmish's installation had failed—smarmy words for, if Fountain Company had killed them—the judges and the Company would have picked another criminal. That meant a train would have been put into service twice in quick succession, in Savda or nearby, when Ise was Mirek's age or a little younger.

Trains had names and numbers and their own patterns on their eyes. Ise didn't even need to be a Fountain heir to check the data. There were albums.

The search was slower than they expected, because a train that had had two souls was a train that had had two names. But Ise knew their engines, knew the difference between a Samikh-Lamid One and Two. Lamid Threes were rare, and if Savda had produced a pair of them, in quick succession, in the year that Ise was learning how to write—that was the engine that had killed Tohmish.

Ise fell asleep at their desk, wondering what to do. The next day, lacking other inspiration, they hiked up the mountain. It was cold, even going straight up. They should have worn a thicker coat.

They were rewarded for their fecklessness by an owl nestled in a tuft of grasses. Its wings were speckled with brown, but its face was the white of fresh-fallen snow. So were the undersides of its wings, when it startled and launched. The snow owls had arrived early. Though perhaps not so very early—the air felt thick around Ise, and they knew if they didn't scramble down the hillside soon they'd be disoriented in the clouds.

Ise told Tohmishevet at tea there might be snow. They covered over all their questions and their fears with stories: the times the whole household had been trapped by snow for days, the way the house grew warm when snow coated it, the time the head of staff took a sledge down to the station and returned with plums and cheese. They slept early, not intending to.

Ise woke to an alarm that said Tohmishevet was leaving. She had called a kab from the tiny town by the train station.

Ise wasted precious seconds persuading the house that the middle of the night was a fine time for target practice. At last they extracted their pistol from its safe, loaded it, and cut through the south wing. They stood with their back to the front door, the door that nobody ever used save guests and Mother, gripped their pistol in both hands, shoved the safety back with their thumb, and waited.

Tohmishevet had discarded her veils. She wore a plain black stocking cap and carried a single case—the one for books, not the one for clothes.

"I found the train that killed your parent," Ise told her.

Tohmishevet smiled a centuries-dead ghost of her usual smile, shifting her grip on the case. "You are a very resourceful person."

"I know what kind of person I am!" Wrong. Cold. Ise had to stay cold. "Put the suitcase down."

Ise tracked the center of their tutor's body as she bent, placing her books neatly at her side, and stood again.

"Step away."

There was only so far to step, in the narrow hall, but Tohmishevet complied.

Ise's left palm was beginning to ache—that hand was still not as strong as the other—but they could shift into an easier stance, now they weren't worried about books flying at them. "What was your parent's crime?"

"Embezzlement," Tohmishevet said crisply, in the way she resolved a statistical conundrum.

Knots and wires. Ise hadn't realized, until the tension wrapped them up again, how badly they'd been hoping that Tohmish-who-was was innocent. That Tohmishevet was an avenger out of legend, setting free those who should never have been bound. What a simplistic way of looking at the world. Even Mirek, small as he was, had no innocence at all.

"Tell me why?" Ise had meant a directive, but their voice lifted. They compensated with a glare.

"Accountancy is a skill of people, not of numbers. You relay what your tablet tells you, putting a human face on the inevitable. And like many other skills of human care, nobody wants to pay what it is worth. My brother had to post a safety bond, in his first position. My parent borrowed the funds from a client's escrow account, and didn't put them back in time."

"Somebody should have done something! There should have been"—who did you have, when you didn't have a household full of staff?— "an association of the miners."

"But there wasn't. There was only my brother and me, and we were not enough." Tohmishevet nodded, managing to create the impression of a bow without moving her hands at all. "Ise, may I leave? My kab is waiting."

"You can't go," Ise told her. Because they had given their word, and because in the dim light of the sleeping house it seemed inevitable, they explained, "If you do, Mother will send Nurse away."

"She'll fire Ndahi?" Tohmishevet asked, startled.

Tohmishevet had spoken all of ten words to Nurse. Ise knew, because they had watched all the footage. The two women were not friends. Ise would not even have sworn that their tutor knew Nurse's surname, and Mirek always referred to Nurse as Nurse. If Tohmishevet knew Nurse's nickname, which held the roll of wheels across the steppes—

Everyone knew that the steppe rovers and the Fishercats worked together. Ise just hadn't expected to see the weave so close. "Mother told me she would fire Nurse, if you left before the year was out," they confirmed. "And then Nurse's joints would puff up like galls on oaks. I have to keep her safe."

"Ise, your house is recording everything we say. Do you know what will happen to me, if I stay? And to your Nurse, as well?"

Ise was their father's child. They could splice a bit of footage. "I can fix it."

But in doing so, they would hurt somebody, somewhere, in a way they couldn't anticipate. Ise always fucked things up eventually. It was the knot of their life. They were the child of both their parents, everything they knew how to do came from the house, and the house was sustained by Fountain Company. Fountain Company sewed people up with wires and never, ever let them go.

Except—except that Tohmishevet had a pocket full of manuals on how to get somebody out. All you needed was a way to support people as they woke up. If you had that, you could unpick all the strands, smooth them out and let people breathe free. And Ise—Ise could do more than change the house recordings. "Scholar Tohmishevet. If you stay, I will help you steal Mother's healing accelerator."

Tohmishevet stared at them, her eyes wide and unreadable in the dim light, and then she laughed. "Ise, look away."

"I can't."

"Green saint, I'm not going to jump you now. You can look down for a minute and a half."

Ise moved their pistol's safety back into position, dropped the muzzle, and settled their shoulders against the doors. They watched the shadows at their feet; they heard a rustling.

"All right." Tohmishevet held her hand out, palm up. In it there was four centimeters of ribbon, the color of oiled steel. "Is it a bargain?"

Ise clasped her hand, the hand full of Fishercat ribbon, and noticed that her nails were painted black. "I give you my word, as an heir to Fountain Company."

They were going to remake the braid.

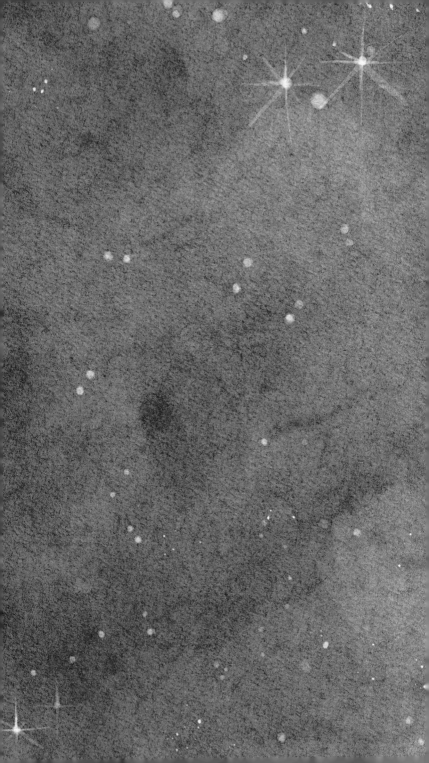

A Fisher of Stars

in the year 3382 of the Nakhorian reckoning

BEFORE I BECAME a starship, I grew their bones. Or spun them, or mined them—I used to think of it as making jaggery candy. I had a swarm of drones in those days. They pulled a substance like soft caramel out of the thin spots between our universe and the Deep; the shock of vacuum snapped it into hardness.

My job was to monitor. Sometimes I'd take a skiff on a lazy spiral round the drones and bones, and on one memorable occasion I had to hook a drone out manually to repair its arm. But I spent most of my time in the tiny bubble of our satellite-station, watching the screens. I was responsible for my entire swarm: if one needed to slant or turn aside, it was my duty to give the command.

The Company had put three of us on that bubble-station: at any given time, one of us was doing chores or grinding through a weights routine, one was working, and one was sleeping. We didn't talk much. My university friends, who knew me when I started every day at a teashop drinking tea and ended every day at another teashop drinking vodka, would not have recognized me. But that was the point. I'd spent all of my life fulfilling others' expectations, being the student and the friend who always came when called. I'd wanted to know who I was when I was by myself.

I got it wrong, of course. Everyone does, when they're in their twenties. But I got it more wrong than most: that's why I'm a starship.

After I had spent half a year inside the bubble-station, I was granted my first leave. An advocate wouldn't measure it this way, but I know: that's when my crime started. An in-system tug brought me to Nakharat Main Station. I shouldered my single bag and joined the queue of people waiting for the elevator.

Nawri was in the queue. I knew him from training. He was about my height, another small round-cheeked North Continent person; his mustache was only the faintest shadow. I dropped back a couple places in line, until I stood beside him, and asked him what his plans were for his leave.

He shrugged. "Go to Khaniqalet, see the Museum of the Book, find true love?"

"Divine inspiration will provide you with a man?"

"Or at least a good time! What about you, Aizu? Are you looking for a girlfriend?"

"All I want is flatbread that doesn't taste like spray-foam."

I wouldn't find it on the elevator. Our particular car was named Chinuyat—a North Continent name, which I assumed meant luck of some kind. (You can judge for yourself whether it was good or ill.) The car had four decks, and every person packed into it was allocated one bunk and four drink tickets per day.

I spent my tickets on papaya juice. I spent the journey rolling its sweetness on my tongue and staring out the window, waiting for the moment when the planet would swap from looking like a toy to looking like a world. Of course, I missed it. One minute it shown like a light-emitting diode through a frosted filter, and the next I was looking at vast crumpled mountains.

As we got closer to our destination, the world shone again. The desert was full of mirror arrays, turning to catch the light. Nawri and I joked that the flashes encoded messages for us. By then, we were best friends. It was that or hate each other, and we were too giddy for hatred.

The station at the bottom of the elevator had vaulted ceilings and tiles the soft gold of a lily stamen. The air was hot and dry, almost as dry as the station up above. We jostled past kiosks selling bottled water and elevator-pattern scarves, looking for the train.

"Look," Nawri said. "That person, and their friend—they have the right idea."

I followed the line of his gaze. He could only mean two people, out of all the crowd. They were cutting toward the exit as if they were the current and all the other people merely flotsam. But what Nawri had noticed was that they had shrugged out of their heavy Company-issue coveralls, and were wearing wide-sleeved, airy tunics. Nawri was watching the taller of the two—though both were tall, even in this crowd—who had a turban woven with a nesting arrow pattern. I looked at the woman. The fabric flowed over her shoulders like a breeze that didn't exist.

Someone was going to trip over Nawri if he didn't start moving. I nudged him out the door and prompted him through the ticket-machine's myriad demands for identification, snagging us seats on a train named Erasil. In choreography as arduous as docking my entire swarm of drones, I brought us to the same train-car as the people we had admired. I dawdled for a moment, debating whether to

take my tablet from my bag. Thus, when the train started
moving, it was natural for us to take seats facing backward.
We were across from the turbaned person and their friend:
that had all the inevitability of fate.

Once we were settled, I asked, "Are you from Khaniqalet?"

The turbaned person—I might as well tell you now,
their nickname was Bira—laughed. Their face was all
angles, with a squared-off chin. When they were laughing,
everything reversed: eyes squeezing shut, mouth round.

"We're from the other side of the continent," their
friend Rayet explained. "It's raining back home.
Everywhere you step is a puddle or a vine-leaf." Her
brows were thick. She hadn't shaped them in the
conventional fashion, but her lips were as bright as a flare.

"The frogs boom like thunder?" Nawri asked.

Rayet made an interrogative noise.

"It's a poet I like. 'The frogs boom like thunder, their
backs are a map'?" He was looking down, regretting the
explanation.

"Their poison is 'a map of lightning never striking'! You
know the Fraying Cord Poet?" Bira leaned forward, reeling
off other epithets: the Poet Who Saw the Saint Sleeping, the
Poet Who Takes By the Hand. Nawri capped each with a
line of verse. The two showed no sign of pausing.

"Well," I asked Rayet, "do you like Nine Pebbles?"

We balanced my tablet between us and began to play,
flicking gem upon gem into an imaginary treasury. By the
time our train reached the outskirts of Khaniqalet, I owed
Rayet two drinks, she had recommended a hostel, and
Nawri had bashfully confessed to writing poetry himself.

All four of us went together to see the Museum of the
Book. Bira and I arranged it: despite their bookishness,
they had a knack for bending the world to do as they
wished. All the buildings in the historic part of Khaniqalet
were made of white marble, sheened blue by indigenous
bacteria-symbionts, which grew where nothing else could.

Most of those compounds were law-courts, with a white-wigged judge hunched over a desk at the center, as a virus curls inside the nucleus of a cell. In the center of all the law-courts shone the museum, falsely cool, with a huge gate.

The Book itself was very small: the size of Rayet's two hands, hinged together. The text looked like vertical stripes, columns defined by the stem-line, more texture than letters. But these were words: words as the Fourth Prophet had recited them, words that the Nakhorians had preserved, through all our wanderings in the Deep.

I must beg for your forgiveness. I don't remember the verse. The incomprehensible calligraphy is no excuse, since the same text was posted all around the room, reshaped and magnified. I remember Rayet turning her head to read it. Miraculously, despite all our walking in the sun, the pleats of her headscarf were still crisp.

The verse was something about the axioms of the Divine. Inevitability, approximations to perfection—they clearly had the museum in mind, as an approach to perfect. People in Khaniqalet were arrogant as fuck.

When we weren't playing tourist, we drank. We toasted with brandy and we toasted with vodka. Bira memorized some of Nawri's verse. I figured out Rayet's system for placing salt-licks, and beat her at Nine Pebbles four times in a row.

But the judges of Khaniqalet, in their infinite wisdom, had decided excessive drunkenness was a public hazard. They decreed an additive for all the vodka in the teashops, so as you drank more you grew more sober, and after six toasts it was as if you'd drunk nothing at all. Nawri was allergic to hashish, which made the student's usual alternative seem less fun. He had not, to the best of my knowledge, kissed Bira yet. They hovered about each other, never quite touching.

At last I asked, "What do you *do* in Khaniqalet, when you've been to the Museum of the Book, and can't get drunk?"

Bira grinned lopsidedly. "Get married?"

Why not? They had the judges to solemnize any number of vows. It would be interesting to see a wedding. Cultural. I could feel all of us thinking that it was possible, that we had been growing closer and closer together. All it took was one bold action, to define a future.

I was the person who spoke aloud what everybody thought, so I raised my vodka glass in a fruitless toast, asking, "Why not?"

Rayet laughed in startlement.

"I mean it," I said. "Why not? We can draw lots, and the two losers can go before a judge."

We found a velvet bag. Inside it, we placed two white stones from one set of Nine Pebbles for the winner, and two blue stones from another set for loss. I handed the bag to Bira first. I saw them shake it back and forth, and curl their fingers. They handed the bag to Nawri, and I smiled, trusting in their gift for arranging the world. I was next, and Rayet last. But by then, the outcome had been determined. It was waiting for us.

We bumped our four fists together, above the empty toasting-glasses, then turned to cupped palms. My hand held a blue stone. I paused for a long second, looking at Bira. I saw their slow smile, and realized they had arranged the world exactly as they wanted.

Then there was nothing for it but to hug Rayet, my fiancée. Our limbs collided awkwardly, and my chest was so hot my stomach hurt. When we disentangled ourselves, we saw Bira and Nawri clasping hands, grinning in sympathy and relief.

We went to a law-court with a grand facade and modules of rooms as snarled as a student's circuit board. The steps were covered with people posing; the corridors were hushed. The clerk who took our names had wrapped his stylus in an ergonomic rubber grip, like a child learning to write.

The judge looked like my youngest aunt. She had the judge's wig, that timeless pale cascade that admits no obligation, and the West Continent air of being much too grand and busy for the small room she was sitting in. But like my aunt, she wore too many rings, and also like my aunt, she talked with her hands, clicking the rings together to emphasize her certainty. She told us about her lineage as a scholar and her mentors in judgeship and she made each of us state our name and place of birth. Just as I was beginning to think that getting married was like visiting a new physician, she clapped her hands, so not only her rings but all her bracelets jangled together, and asked, "How long is the contract?"

Rayet and I exchanged glances. Rayet seemed unusually tentative. She was offering me a last chance to regret. But I didn't want to. I didn't want her to think she was an impulse or a bad holiday decision. That would have been insulting. A year and a day seemed almost as bad.

I could have said four years, or eight, or a dozen years and months and days. But I was young, so young that at every step I felt I could bounce away from the planet, weightless, and a dozen years felt like a less complimentary version of forever. I couldn't imagine forever with Rayet. But I wanted to. I said, "A permanent contract."

Rayet tucked her chin in the tiny nod that meant, "I am winning this round," and also, "Yes."

The judge was too professional to react with her face, but her rings clashed like a cliff-face falling. "Very well. Then you will seal the register"—she used Bira and Nawri's full names, which in the press of years I have forgotten—"and step outside." That left Rayet and me, waiting to unveil.

I don't know if you have ever been married. I hope, for your spouse's sake, that you have not. But likely, if you have, it developed slowly. Long kisses. Embraces in the dark. One finger slipped beneath a scarf to touch the edge of a braid.

I saw all of Rayet's vows at once, every commitment she had made, woven with glints and sheen into the thick braids of her hair. She stared back at me, her pupils dark and wide.

I will not tell you how many ribbons she had, nor of what colors, for to the best of my knowledge she is still alive. But I can tell you the cord they use for marriage in the halls of Khaniqalet is the thick orange of the center of an egg. When I tried to twist it into Rayet's hair, I nearly dropped it, and she caught my wrist with a laugh.

We went on laughing, all that day and into the night, as we folded ourselves into a narrow hostel bed and tried to see the future. I wanted to design starships; Rayet wanted to run a space station. We plotted her career as an administrator, my transfer to Rosemallow Company with her, a planetary interlude where I'd earn an advanced degree and she would make friends with judges. I learned that when she was close to ecstasy she called on the first settlers of Nakharat. Her tongue touched her lower lip when she came.

Data transfer between bubble-stations was strictly metered, so when Rayet and I went back to work, we sent letters that were all voice and no pictures. When I ran out of things to say about my daily routine, I started sharing memories: sledding down the piles of snow mounded next to the light-rail station, the time my university flatmate tried cultivating planetary algae. The way my milk-father built two-stringed guitars. I sang a couple of my second father's songs, very softly.

At any volume, I would have scared the other bubble-station workers. None of us played music: there was a Cypress Company rule against playing music at volume, while we were on station. The cynical said the rule curried favor with strict judges. The rest of us said music was asking for bad luck. If you sang too long to the bones of starships, something might try to answer.

Rayet didn't snap at me when she answered my letter. But she didn't ask about my fathers, either.

We spent our first few leave periods together, wrapped up so tightly that we barely broke for tea. But soon Rayet was promoted to coordinator. After that, our schedules fell out of sync. We sent even more letters—and then, somehow, fewer and fewer. When I piloted my skiff through the drone swarm, I no longer narrated the adventure to an imaginary Rayet. Instead a song ran through my head—"No, we're not a pair of lovebirds, I cannot decrypt this message"— with the gleeful, bouncing rhythm folk songs always have.

The other reason I didn't write to Rayet was, I was getting sick.

At first, I could dismiss the twinges and prickles as mechanical. I spent too much time hunching over screens. I had been skimping on my weight routine. I needed to stretch. But after a while I could feel a pulsing, a ripple of pain that started at my toes and shuddered through my body. I might have hummed to it, "I cannot decrypt this message." The rhythms matched.

The pain was stronger when I was out in my skiff, up against the bones of future ships. I thought sometimes I could feel them vibrating, in tune with the stabbing that danced along my nerves and the song stuck in my head.

You know how easy it is to sync up with a starship's spine. You know how much it hurts to burst out of the Deep, into the pressure of ordinary space and time. Imagine, then, what it feels like to be trapped at the interface.

I only caught the echo of it, and I thought that I would shake myself apart.

I daydreamed about accelerating the bone growth, ripping the shards free. Launching myself back to the planet with wings stretched over fragments from the Deep. It was a childish, unaerodynamic wish. I might as well have slammed into the atmosphere with a burning paper glider.

The accident, when it came, was much simpler.

We were building a junction. Think of it as a diver opening her arms wide, or as curling ribs, if you would rather think of bone. The arms already spread in ordinary space. We were drawing out the longer piece, drones hovering around it, alert for any variation in hue or gravitational fingerprint that might indicate a flaw.

My skiff was orbiting the end of the sunward junction arm when a wave of pain crashed through my body and back again, echoing up from my toes. I tried to breathe into it, relaxing my muscles so the drone haptics wouldn't react. But when I opened my eyes, the whole junction was spinning, great arms twirling in an ungainly pirouette. The thread into the Deep must have snapped. A drone could have snapped it.

I shoved the skiff's control stick up, slewing around to hover where the dancer's head should have been, while I issued commands to the drones. *Observe. Report. Stabilize.* I didn't see the wobble near the lost attachment point. I was experienced enough that I should have expected it, all the same. I should have known the whole huge piece could flip.

The spine slammed into my skiff. My body thrummed, alarms keened all around me, and then the skiff was skipping outward while the junction went on spinning.

I shoved the control stick again. The skiff lagged and swerved. It felt like sliding over thick-packed snow, if you could skid while falling up. An alarm repeated, intentionally out of sync. I didn't recognize the stars above me.

I wanted to call my drones, but the haptics told me they were balanced perfectly around the junction. Any rearrangement would disrupt the fragile chance of stabilization. Four drones were free, though. They hung back near the bubble-station, reserved to guide an evac suit, in case the bubble popped.

If I took those drones and the emergency spread, my bubble-mates would be trapped. If I didn't take them, I might be able to bend the skiff's path toward a station farther down the line. Or I might skew away from human-frequented coordinates until my air ran out.

I dropped the skiff's nose as far as I could and called the backup drones.

I spent the investigation that followed sipping water. My throat burned with half-swallowed acid, like I had gargled sand. My bubble-mates were kind to me, referencing practical responses and presence of mind, but I knew that if debris had pierced our station, they would have been left adrift. Debris had been out there, even before the junction snapped. The investigators found a mangled piece of metal wedged inside the siphon to the Deep.

The Company offered me a remedial course on safety procedures and a new posting. I waited a quarter of a year, till the investigators filed their final report. Then I notified medical personnel of the hum along my bones. Eight days later, I had a tiny pension and a one-way ticket.

I bought a pair of scissors in the elevator terminal, hid in one of the tiny shower-stalls, and cut my hair. My Cypress Company braid was narrow and the strands parted easily. I had to hack at my marriage braid, pulling it taut and hearing the cord split with a crunch. I stuffed it into the recycler chute and snipped my other braids to match. The teahouse where my university friends had gathered, the thank-you from the boy I used to tutor, my cousin's marriage-favor—these all belonged to someone who no longer existed.

I used one metered burst of water to rinse the stray hairs off my neck, then wrapped my scarf around a child-light head.

You've probably guessed: I never wrote to Rayet.

I didn't go back to the city I grew up in. I didn't want to see the mountains. Instead, I found a pair of rooms in the basement of a Demalat skyscraper, smack dab in the center of North Continent. There was nothing on the horizon except steppe and wheat. I bought a mattress that unrolled in the evening and rolled up again in the morning, and after some searching, I managed to adopt a lizard-dog.

Lizard-dogs aren't popular in cities, or on North Continent. They're too big and too carnivorous for a family flat, and most of them hate stairs. But I loved the patterns in Buribak's scales, like sun on desert hills, and the fanned limbs he spread to cool and warm himself. I didn't mind that he would sleep all winter. I thought that I might do the same.

When the days grew long again and all the snow was melted, after I finally managed to re-roll my mattress three days in a row, Buribak and I started going to the park. It was a boring city park with a fence around the edge and a broken fountain. Small children crawled over the play structure, some in batches with colored nursery armbands, some watched by individual tutors. Then there were fluffy portable dogs, like ducklings with too many legs, and their elderly owners, bundled up in padded coats.

There was one other person old enough to make a contract. The first thing I noticed about her was that she didn't wear a scarf. Once in a museum I got to touch a shell, from one of the few ocean creatures that evolved on Nakharat. It looked as soft as a peach without fuzz. Her skin had that quality, like it might dimple under your thumb, or it might be distilled rock.

The second thing I noticed was, her dog was bounding straight for Buribak.

Buribak's fans snapped out and he started humming, low and weird. I swung my coat wide, making myself even bigger, and chirped at him to stay. Meanwhile, the other dog was bouncing and yelping. It was taller than Buribak at the shoulder, all triangles and enthusiasm, and the fifth or sixth time the woman called its name, it actually listened. Buribak and I shook ourselves back to normal size. My shoulders were stinging.

The woman was still holding her dog's collar. It was not taller than her at the shoulder, but the competition was close. "I regret the disturbance," she told me, with the proud and embarrassed smile common to pet owners across the universe. "Kotzha and I both regret it. I'm Ulmeket."

"Thanks," I said. "This is Buribak. We should be going."

She looked at both of us with friendly interest, her eyes resting more on me than on my pet. "May I ask you something?"

"If you don't expect me to answer." I wasn't trying to make it a joke.

"I wouldn't, it is private information!" Just as I was asking myself what she thought lizard-dogs were, she added, "How much is your pension?"

I was so shocked I gave her the number. My brain caught up enough to point out it was obvious, that two people our age wouldn't be childless in the park mid-morning for any other reason. I wasn't fast enough to stop myself from asking, "How much is yours?"

Ulmeket's pension was more than mine, but barely so. I congratulated her, wondering if she was also sick. She laughed without self-consciousness, Kotzha rubbing against her hand.

Before I left the park, Ulmeket had invited me to a Fourthday evening study group. To my own surprise, I went.

The group was, inevitably, religious. Only student-advocates or the devout would choose to study on a Fourthday. I hoped for Nawri's style of piety, all mystic references and flirtation, though I felt too old and broken for the latter. I feared I would meet a group of would-be judges poring over commentaries on the Book to find new things to outlaw.

Ulmeket's friends were a new thing in my experience.

They were genuinely devoted to doing good. They had
a favorite verse—something about how two people who
share a plate of dumplings have read the Book together—
and they used to recite it, pass around a dish of millet
sweets, and then report on their efforts of the past week.
There was a woman who could not stop bragging and a
person who could not sweeten their tea without advice.
You find people like them in every group. But I was
startled how often somebody made sense.

The group's efforts often fell in the sticky ground
between the judges' rostered charities and the kindnesses
of friends. Anyone in Demalat could go to a municipal
cafeteria and find soup and bread. But if you wanted
more personal help, aid cleaning your home or a nursery
place for your child, you had to join a city ward. If you
owned property or held a lease in your own name, this
was automatic. For anyone else, joining a ward was a
maze of oaths and seals. The study group sponsored ward
memberships and held mending days. We fixed the sound
on people's tablets and figured out how to make printers
print. But more than anything else, the study group
offered babysitting.

Ulmeket was a phenomenal babysitter. She was short
and her face was very round, so adults sometimes assumed
she was a child herself. Children never made this mistake.
Instead, they begged for songs and stories. Ulmeket could
convert songs into action: she would hum and clap her
hands, and suddenly kids would be racing past each other
to find the prettiest bug or pick up bits of trash. I tried to
clap along sometimes. It sent bits of fizz along my bones,
half needles and half joy.

That summer, we were at a picnic for the Demalat
Railway Workers Association. Buribak sprawled in the tall
grass like a bronze statue of a flower. Ulmeket was playing
a game with the little kids involving tubs of brightly
colored water. The bigger kids were playing Train.

I don't know what part of Nakharat you're from, so I don't know if you have played Train. We all did, on North Continent, when we were small. In Khaniqalet, they thought it was irreligious. Train starts like a normal tag game, with all the children running after each other, but the first child caught freezes with their eyes closed and their arms flung out. They're the engine. Anyone who touches the engine, or is shoved into them or "arrested" and dragged up to them, has to join the chain. These kids were the children of railway workers and also dramatic, so at the end of the game they held a ceremony where the engine yelled, "My name is so-and-so and I'm repenting of my crime!"

"They never tell us the names," said the parent standing next to me.

I looked at him more carefully. There was beer foam on his mustache, but he didn't seem severely drunk. Just appreciating the picnic. "Have you lost someone?" I asked.

He had, and if I hadn't spent the winter curled around my own pain, I would have known it. Someone fucked up the plowing and let ice cake near the tracks. In the subsequent derailment, two railway inspectors were killed.

"I had known the senior inspector since I was my daughter's age," he said, gesturing. "And they wouldn't tell us. They wouldn't tell us who it was."

Humans were supposed to take responsibility for human life. What good was it to embed a convict in an engine, if you couldn't blame them for the crash? But Fountain Company said identifying individual trains would encourage subversive elements.

Ulmeket glanced up from her tubs of water. "Company shareholders hate following their own rules."

"That sounds personal," I said, startled.

"I knew a child once who tried to make me sign a nondisclosure contract after he broke a vase."

"And did you?"

She tucked her scarf behind her ear, the way women do when they're thinking of a braid. A toddler began clutching their face with green hands in imitation, and out on the field a bigger child stumbled. I thought my chance to hear the story was lost.

In the teashop that evening, the bragging woman explained her plan for a railway workers' protest. They should demand improved city plowing, or even better, Fountain Company should purchase new plows. Inspectors should fill out a fourfold checklist before going near the tracks.

"Will these changes come quickly?" asked the person who could not sweeten their tea on their own.

"If the Demalat Association stands firm!"

"It sounds so simple, when your job's not on the line." I spoke in an undertone, just to Ulmeket, but I instantly regretted my words. At least her friends had something to wish for.

She reached for the sugarbowl, turning away from the crowd. "Even if it works, we're only one city."

"Of course we're in a city." The alternative was to join a Company enclave, the planetary versions of my bubble-station. Or you could farm. Army wheat if you were conventional, goats if you were eccentric.

She shook her head quickly, crinkling her veil. "But we could think of all the cities. Or the railway workers could."

"A whole continent at a time?" The way I hadn't thought of myself as North Continent, until I left.

"Or all the continents. That's how the Companies think."

I saw her look upward, remembering something. I risked asking, "How did you learn that? How Companies think?"

She shook herself, still partway into memory. "He loved plushworms."

I thought she meant a lover, and I thought that I shouldn't mind if she did, so I asked the safer question: "What's a plushworm?"

"Oh! They're sea creatures. So many spines that they seem soft. Toxic, but not venomous."

"Did he have an aquarium?"

"Nobody gives a five-year-old a seawater aquarium, not even shareholders."

I laughed. I should have known Ulmeket would be focused on the children. "I see how you learned plushworm facts. But how did you meet this boy's family?"

She said, fast and tight, "I was his nurse."

I thought of my own father, holding me close and joking the induction drug tasted like burnt roses. "Your nurseling's parents must have been so sad, when the milk wouldn't come. I'm glad they found you."

"That's what I thought at first. But then I realized it was easier for them to pay somebody else."

"Hellstars, that is cold."

"Yeah. Metal railings at midwinter, that kind of cold. But I miss him anyway."

I hugged her, the way I would hug any friend who was sad. She hugged me back, cautious and gentle. From her care, I recognized two things: this was not the same as it would be with any other friend, and it was more than a year since I'd touched anyone at all.

I knew Ulmeket had felt me tense, so I offered her a truth. "The music in here hurts. I like it, but it scrapes under my skin and along my finger bones."

She listened for the melody, behind the clink of glasses and the cheerful arguments. "Should we go?"

"I'll be all right," I said automatically. "I am. All right."

Ulmeket straightened, pulling her feet off the rungs of the bench and resting them squarely on the floor. "I did make an agreement with his parents, in the end. I can't work for another family. That's why they pensioned me."

In her bluntness, I recognized a trade: truth for truth, pain for pain. "Do you ever hear from the child?"

"No. But with the pension, I could be anything."

"It's awfully empty, being anything."

Ulmeket shivered and set her hand near mine, cautious of my pain. "I see different pieces now, of what people need." She was donning a purpose, as if shrugging her arms into a heavy robe.

That wasn't the night we agreed we would be lovers. We spent another half-year circling round each other; my braids fell past my shoulders, when she finally touched them. But it's the night we always counted from, in retrospect.

Moving my things to Ulmeket's place was embarrassingly easy. I fretted more about Buribak and Kotzha, but they discovered that Buribak could lift a puzzle-box with his snout and rattle it with his fins until all the food fell out, and after that Kotzha followed him around with cautious adoration.

If you weren't already out here, you'll remember the next summer. The heat slammed into you with the subtlety of a four-year-old grown as tall as a Company tower. I recognized the feeling from my time on West Continent. But on West Continent they built for that sort of weather. Demalat was designed for long, cold winters. Its buildings cradled heat. City fountains ran dry. The street-cleaners went on strike. Old people fell asleep and never woke up.

A train died, too. The system that kept its conscience lulled and waiting overheated, and the train ground to a halt, shutting down the line. I wish I had grieved that death, of all the deaths around me, but instead all I could think was that I had finally agreed to introduce Ulmeket to my fathers, and I had failed. I hauled myself to my feet—we had already claimed a bench at the station, when they started canceling the trains—and sighed so loud it was almost a song.

Ulmeket put her arm around me to take the yogurt drink we were sharing. Condensation formed on the bottle in perfect half-spheres. Ulmeket's sweat was like that, too. Self-contained droplets. "It'll be all right. Kotzha and Buribak will be delighted, to see us back so soon. Then next year, when we are married—" Her sly smile faltered. Even Ulmeket could be afraid to make a joke too real.

But I was the one who spoke aloud what everyone was thinking, so I said, "You're right. When it is cold again, we will get married."

I didn't feel guilty. I didn't realize that I could feel guilty until weeks later, and even then it felt muted. Like a philosophical puzzle. Another woman had visited the courts of Khaniqalet, long ago and far away.

We did all the traditional wedding things—the meeting with the genetic counselor, a formal dinner with Ulmeket's mother and with my fathers. We held a celebratory breakfast for our association of volunteers and bought new collars for Buribak and Kotzha. My youngest aunt raised her eyebrows when she heard we planned a permanent contract, but everyone else took it as a matter of course. In their minds, our permanence was already established.

After the wedding, Ulmeket and I started trying to get pregnant. I thought it would be straightforward, and I suppose my part was: a few injections, a quiet afternoon in the neighborhood health center. But Ulmeket would be carrying our child.

In school, when they told us that without implants many people bleed every twenty-eight days, on the schedule of some galaxy-distant moon, I assumed the twenty-eight days was literal. In truth it was the kind of average invented by a hopeful project manager. We were constantly monitoring, watching hormone levels and applying drug patches, till I wished for miniaturized versions of my old drone swarm.

I got a letter from Nawri on one of the mornings that Ulmeket was at the health center. It was a real letter, written on cotton paper in a swirling hand. It seemed entirely out of place at a park full of dogs. Nawri was doing well. He had transferred to Bira's Company, and Bira had been promoted. They were trying out a four-year marriage contract, to see how they liked it. Rayet had been promoted too, to deputy administrator. He wasn't sure how things were between us, but perhaps I would want to congratulate her? And he had almost forgotten to mention that he was a runner-up in a continent-wide poetry contest, with a poem that for once was neither about rain nor stars.

Intercontinental mail was slow; Nawri would be back on station. I sent him a quick voice message celebrating the contract and the poem, and planned to send a longer message later, when I knew what I wanted to say.

Ulmeket came back from her appointment serene in the confidence that this time, one of our embryos was growing. A few days later, the monitor bracelet on her left wrist began glowing green, in gentle agreement. I sorted vitamins for Ulmeket and other vitamins for Buribak. I didn't trust the monitor. There were too many ways for life to end in a hostile environment, too many branching paths to failure. I hid checklists where I thought Ulmeket wasn't looking.

I took Kotzha outside early on the morning that things did go wrong. There was a line of pain along each of my ribs, prickling like burrs trapped under my skin, so I didn't go back to bed. That meant I was awake to hear Ulmeket say, "Oh. That looks like blood."

We were barefoot in the bathroom, staring at several distinct clots, when the flat's system chimed. I tugged my early-morning cap on and ran to the door. There were two people waiting, a youngish clerk attempting a bushy beard and a woman in a fashionable stole with wide yellow and narrow red stripes.

I told Kotzha to stay and stepped into the hall. "Is this some sort of survey?"

"This is a legal notification." The clerk tapped his satchel, which must contain a formal document.

The woman asked, "Are you sure you want to do this in the corridor?"

I gazed at her stole. The red was brilliant, a flower shade. It reminded me of the piping on Rayet's Rosemallow Company uniforms. Not like blood at all. I lied, "The dogs won't like you."

"Very well. Do you confirm that you are Aizuret Yerikevet, pensioner of Cypress Company?"

"I am."

The clerk pulled out a tablet and began to read aloud. A blinking light on the upper edge indicated that his words were being entered into the court record. The preamble was long, long enough for me to pretend that this was the kind of problem that could be sorted with an accountant or an advocate, though where we would find the funds to hire one, I didn't know. It was also long enough for Ulmeket to find trousers and slippers and open the door. That meant she was listening as the clerk read, "Aizuret Yerikevet, on behalf of the judicial office of Khaniqalet, I notify you that you stand in breach of contract, having fulfilled neither the duties nor the obligations of a spouse."

"You have the wrong Yerikevet," Ulmeket said firmly. "Aizu is my wife."

The woman smiled a Company smile, her teeth glittering like separate chips of ice. "Perhaps this Yerikevet will come to the local judge's office, as we sort everything out?"

I told Ulmeket, "Make sure Buri gets enough calcium."

She hugged me with a firmness that pretended she could handle everything. "I'll make myself some tea."

I could have whispered that I loved her then. I was already condemned of bigamy, by observation of two witnesses and the Demalat judicial ledgers.

The featherweight of further evidence would have changed nothing. But Ulmeket was a woman who spoke huge truths aloud. I had failed her too deeply to ask for her forgiveness, so deeply that I hadn't even noticed Nawri's warning.

"Tea is a good idea," I said. I let the clerk and the Rosemallow representative lead me away.

The judge who ruled on my conviction was elderly and thin. He hunched under his white wig as if he hoped it was a blanket and told me to uncover my head before sentencing. A woman clerk examined my hair. She touched it gently, confirming there was no ribbon for Rayet. I thought I should have blushed, but I could barely turn my head.

The judge informed me I could redeem my lies as the conscience of a ship or train or elevator car. His clerks imposed a series of tests, blinking lights at the edge of my vision and patterned squeaks and beeps. A person with Company manners but no Company insignia watched the tests, hands folded. They complimented my reflexes and told me that once I was installed in a starship I would fall asleep. I welcomed it: sleep without pain or guilt.

In cases that don't involve the Deep, maybe you do get to rest. But decisions happen fast, when a starship is in danger. Too fast for a human brain, even a brain floating on drugs and threaded with the finest wire. The computer begins feeding your dreaming mind disaster scenarios as soon as your starship starts rising through the Deep. You have to choose. Again and again, you have to choose. Some day, in some possibility, death will be real, and then you must choose right.

Meanwhile, being at the edge of the Deep hurts. I knew it. My nerves were already sensitized. I shuddered awake one day from dreams of collisions and uncontrolled orbits to feel pain along the edges of my bones. It was almost comforting. If my body hadn't hurt, I wouldn't have been sure it still existed.

I was floating near a sun I didn't recognize. It was a little too small and a little too red. I thought, for no good reason, that I smelled hazelnuts. I tried to open my hand and felt a shudder that I recognized, distantly, as the starship beginning insystem maneuvers.

This was like being back on my skiff at the edge of a starship's bone. The smallest motion could become a spin. I breathed deep, through the lungs I couldn't feel, and imagined I was sunlight. The shudder eased. I slipped back into sleep.

After that, I woke more and more frequently. I saw a system where stations scattered across the face of a vast planet the color of summer straw and a system where the sun was ringed with dust. My dreams changed, too. I could feel other ships slipping past me in the Deep. Sometimes I tasted them. The computer would be showing me starships torn apart or fractured in a tidal surge, and I would recognize my neighbor by the eddy in its wake or the sharp taste of black pepper.

There was one ship I saw often. It made me think of heavy cream and currants, pressing my tongue against the top of my palate and feeling a berry burst. In shape it was a freighter, two stacks of bays stuck together with all the grace of a handful of twigs. Easier for skiffs to access, I supposed. I wondered who the person was inside, and what their crime had been.

I was visiting the largest planetoid in the ringed-sun system when the freighter spoke to me. I felt it first as an impulse to wave my hand and whisper a greeting. "Good evening," I thought formally, "Good evening."

Then, after a pause and a slight rotation of the freighter, "Good evening. Can you hear me? I am Makpa."

This could still be a dream. But it was different from any of the disaster scenarios I had dreamed before. The system didn't give other ships women's nicknames.

I imagined speaking slowly and carefully, as if I were initializing a log. "This is Aizuret from Demalat."

My body moved differently when Makpa spoke through it. Shoulders back, arms consciously relaxed, like speaking on a stage. "I am so glad to meet you, Aizuret. How long have you been awake?"

I gave her a count of visited stars and my best guess, from the glimpses I had had of Nakharat and its sun, of how much time had passed. The planetary configurations made it, most likely, three quarters of a year.

Makpa's posture turned inside out, from projecting calm to listening. If we had been chatting in a teashop, she would have tried to drink me in. "You know a lot about navigation."

I confessed—but it didn't feel like a confession, it felt like a reconfiguration, a cloud of twisted decisions reassembling me in this place—"I used to build starships."

We talked for days, as our ships unloaded and reloaded, comparing memories of West Continent and Nakharat and the sensations of traveling between stars. Makpa had never learned my caution about music near the Deep. For her, other starships were not tastes, but sounds: a bell, a cheep, a reverberating growl. She heard me as the whirr of the automatic fan in her childhood home.

We followed different routes, but now that I had met Makpa, I tried talking to every ship I met. Some were not from Nakharat, and thus had no human conscience. Some were not listening. But I met a shy person in a courier ship who struck me as impossibly young, perhaps twenty-four, a gruff woman from South Continent, and a laughing man who claimed my ship felt like the finest grit of sandpaper. Drashu and Girhan were long-range ships, sinking deep even for the Deep. They described stars whose light had never reached as far as Nakharat.

We talked when we met in orbit near Nakharat Main Station, and wherever else we found each other. We learned about each others' families, parents and children, lovers whom we mourned and friends who had betrayed us.

The shy courier told me, haltingly, that they had robbed a string of Amaranth Company rovers at gunpoint, picking them off the tundra one by one. Later I learned Makpa had been an advocate—though ironically, only for civil trials.

I knew we were building something special when Chinuyat began talking to us. At first, I didn't know who she was. I only knew that her sense of her body was strange. Most of us felt stable, when we were in orbit. Chinuyat was almost floating. Wafting, like a seed blown on the wind. That also meant she wasn't in pain. She didn't brace like a person on the surface of the Deep.

Because she wasn't on the surface of the Deep. She wasn't a starship at all. She was one of the elevators.

Chinuyat was older than me, old enough to have grown children and possibly grandchildren, but because she had spent so long dreaming, she felt young. She had been a weaver of ribbons, stretching narrow bands across the ceiling of her flat, writing code to raise and lower a multitude of strands. Somebody hired her for a rush job, a hundred twenty meters in a variant of an old Fountain Company pattern, for the summer fair.

But the pattern wasn't a variant; it was exact. Chinuyat was arrested for forgery. The man who had hired Chinuyat testified at her trial and took the finder's fee. "I should have guessed," she told us. I tasted the hollowness in her whisper, like tea brewed all week on the same leaves.

I felt Makpa leaning forward, gathering attention to her attention. "The guilt does not originate in you. The magistrates need us to fail sometimes, so that they can feel large."

I remembered the judge in Khaniqalet clattering her bracelets, and agreed. Chinuyat's response seemed more like acquiescence. But I thought that Makpa's words would float with her, down the cable to the planet, and up again.

Back at the ringed star, I said to Makpa, "So many of us are from North Continent."

My chest echoed her long sigh, moving out and in, as if we shared ordinary air and not oxygen-charged fluid. "We fought so long."

"You and your clients?" I asked, tentative. The contract negotiations she'd described had sounded more mundane, but I knew she was only sharing fragments of her old life.

"I thought you would have guessed by now." Makpa's words were rapid, without her usual poise. "I was a Fishercat."

Activists, vandals, selfish teenagers, the rot at the center of North Continent, the only association with a moral center—I don't know where your judgment falls. Before I became a starship, I barely thought about the Fishercats, and afterwards, I was too wrapped up in my own misery for philosophical debates. Except—"Last summer, in the heat wave. You were the ones who told us that the trains were dying." The Companies would never have admitted it, on their own. Somebody must have pushed them.

"It worked. It actually worked!" Makpa was all currants now, bursts and explosions of sharpness, unguarded glee. "We planned so long, we thought if we couldn't find a way to communicate we could at least track individuals—and then they caught me."

Makpa had been arrested and convicted, but not, with her smooth-flowing creamy kindness, effectively debriefed. I admired her desperately. I wished I had been so bold. I wished I had come here for a reason.

Then, with the surety of my old swarm of drones aligning, I realized: I *was* an individual, and my pain was mine. I had hurt Ulmeket, and even Rayet, because I refused to look at the whole of who I was. But that debt was mine to pay. The judges didn't deserve it. They shouldn't get to use me.

"We have a way to communicate," I told Makpa.

"With each other, now that we're awake. But if we keep trying—maybe with all of Nakharat."

Makpa and I began talking to the others about associations. I told stories about Ulmeket's group and the dumpling joke. Makpa knew history: the way associations formed on the trading-ships, before Nakhorians came to Nakharat, and the methods the first planet-gardeners used to settle disputes.

"But what is our association for?" asked Drashu. "Lolling about on the lakes and fishing?" They were from the far north of North Continent, originally.

"Fishing in the Deep!" the gruff woman answered.

After that we were the Fishing Association. The link to the Fishercats, or lack thereof, went unspoken. Instead we spread out, trying to talk to others, telling every ship we met that there was an association, and they could join it.

Meanwhile, I picked away at the question of how to speak to people who were not ships or elevators. It was the most frustrating piece of troubleshooting I had ever done, for I had nothing that felt like an interface. The ship's system was a cousin to the haptics I knew well. It fed information to me through subtle shifts in pressure and stimulation of my senses. The sensor networks were impressive. I suspected that my impression of Makpa came in part from the ship's gravity sensors. They were tuned to measure the subtlest change in rifts as we cut into the Deep; they could detect variations in another ship's system. But I couldn't issue commands. The ship only asked me what to do in the event of a disaster.

On the other hand, the ship asked me what to do in the event of a disaster whenever it was in motion. I'd made thousands and thousands of decisions to turn or slow or dive, weighing life against life over and over. I began shifting the instruction: shine a bright light and turn. Shine a bright light and dive. Shine a bright light. Life depends upon that signal.

A day came when my ship rose out of the Deep close to Makpa's and I knew from the rippling joy of her presence that the light shone outside my dreams. She said, quite simply, "I love you."

I panicked. I felt my heart pounding, great thunderous booms that seemed to reverberate through the ship. Distantly, I sensed the crew scrambling. *I can't move,* I told myself. *I can't twitch.* They might be investigating the light.

"Aizu?" asked Makpa.

It would be easy to say what she wanted—what I wanted to tell her. It would be easy to flee into mockery, pretending I was too bitter to care for anything at all. Saying all of what I thought? Even imagining it hurt like the nearness of the Deep, aches rolling through my chest into my spine.

But I knew, by now, how to move through pain. "The first time I was married..." I told Makpa all of it, about Ulmeket and Rayet. By the time I was finished, my crew had worked out how to turn off the shining light and it was possible, somehow, to say, "I love you."

"I'm realizing," she said, "we could be married."

"We can't even hold hands!"

"We don't need to. We don't need judges or even ribbon. A contract is made first between two people." Her certainty was a slow swirl of honey, cut with the sharpness of longing.

What neither of us were saying is that by talking so long to each other, out here at the edge of the Deep, we had already learned each other's bodies. We traced each word by echoing the other's tiniest motions: when I pressed my lips together, she felt it as a kiss. I was committed to Makpa in that moment, in every way a marriage contract formalized.

I could feel how badly she wanted me to say yes. It would be easy to offer her everything. But I couldn't guess who I would become, and this time I knew it. "Let's be married," I agreed, "for four seasons of a year."

Her joy frothed like bubbles in cloud-tinted wine.

When I returned to Nakharat, I marked the planet's position against the stars whose names I knew. Then I asked the other ships what they would ask for, if they could speak to the outside world.

"I would talk to my daughter," said the man who sensed the rest of us as textures, with the impatience of someone asked to add three and four.

"I would ask for new music," said the robber courier ship. They had never learned the superstition of bubble-station life.

That set off a round of reminiscence, comparing memories and families. I talked about my second father's guitar and waited for the conversation to circle back around.

Rising toward the station, Chinuyat mused, "I wish I could read the Book on Fifthday."

When you're adjusting a telescope, there's a moment when a shape turns from a bar-shaped smudge to a pair of stars. We all felt it, the moment when we asked ourselves, how can the judges deny us this?

I knew what everyone wanted to say, and I knew I had made the opportunity to say it: "What if we went on strike?"

At first, I thought the hardest part would be teaching the others how to stop. I knew the components of my ship because I had once built them. When I thought, "The aft engines should not fire," I knew where they were and what that meant. For the others, everything was swaddled in guesswork and nightmare. They'd dreamed over and over again that a wrong move could kill the crew, choking them in vacuum or poisoning them with smoke or stranding them forever in the reaches of the Deep. Now they were trying to find individual systems—have you ever tried to troubleshoot for someone, when you can neither draw a diagram nor gesture toward the part at fault?—and intentionally break them.

But one by one, our ships approached Nakharat Main Station and did not depart. At last Chinuyat, too, paused at the station. I began to broadcast the message we had agreed on: "This is the Fishing Association of starships based at Nakharat. We are the consciences that you have made us. We want to talk."

The station sent a delegation with three members: a senior advocate, a leytenant colonel, and a Company representative. They were flanked by a crew of techs who milled about, trying to open a private communications channel. The techs were also trying to send me back to sleep. A heaviness settled over me, the steel-and-garlic taste of the station growing muddy.

I battled the ship's cameras, trying to bring the delegation into focus. They were clumped near the entrance of the access tube, wearing flexible suits for low-pressure environments, but with their face-masks raised. The leytenant colonel led the way, a ceremonial sword slung over his back. The advocate was fiddling with her gloves. Her suit looked a little too big.

The Company rep had a yellow flower splashed across the left shoulder of her suit, a magenta star at its center. I didn't actually need the Rosemallow logo to cue me. I knew from her stance, the freedom of her sweeping gestures, that it was Rayet.

The old song shuddered through me—"I cannot decrypt this message"—each beat a separate blow. I was awake now. I had never been so awake. I whispered to Makpa, "It's her. My former wife."

"They've researched you," she whispered back. "That means we frightened them."

I resolved to act as if I believed her. That's all that you can do sometimes. Move in the direction that you know is right, and hope your mind catches up.

The techs had a comm channel established at last. I said through it, "Welcome. I regret I cannot offer you a toast, but the judges have made that impossible." It was the best way to signal everything that I regretted.

I saw Rayet's brows draw together in recognition. It was really me, and we were on different sides, playing something far more serious than Nine Pebbles.

I went on to introduce the other ships who had converged on the station, beginning with Makpa and ending with a description of Chinuyat. The advocate listened carefully, her tablet out. I assumed she was recording everything. The army officer looked impatient. Rayet was coiled and waiting.

The Fishing Association had planned this approach. It was important to emphasize that we were an association of equals. But now I saw a secondary advantage. Rayet had a clearer head for strategy than mine, but her patience was finite. If I could draw the process out, she would begin to make mistakes.

At first the delegation said they would forgive us if we went back to work. As hours stretched into days and the elevator remained trapped at the station, they amended their position: they would allow us to send letters approved by a panel of judges. The advocate left off her pressure-suit and began drinking flask after flask of tea.

We had solved Ulmeket's riddle, I realized. The judges, army, and the Companies could not divide city against city when all of us were at the edge of vacuum together.

I had half a season left to be married to Makpa when the delegation made a true counter-proposal. I knew something was different the moment they approached my ship. The leytenant colonel was twice as grim as usual. Rayet smiled wide, her lips the color of the Rosemallow's heart.

The proposal offered a dedicated channel, a way that ships could route messages to and from the ordinary mail. It would be expensive to write to us, but no more expensive than sending any other message between stars. We could have books and music. Ships would have the right to contact a designated advocate.

"And in light of your extraordinary efforts and demonstrated piety," the delegation's advocate said with a professional smile, "a panel of judges has agreed to offer clemency to the eight leaders of your association."

"I can go home?" Chinuyat's astonishment was like spun sugar.

"Thank you," I told the delegation. "We will consider your proposal most carefully."

The association's conversation was a mix of exhilaration and resentment. We were victorious. We had clawed back the tiniest of privileges: even a beleaguered army private had chances to contact family. Some of us were going home.

I could see my family again. I could attempt to play my second father's guitar. I tried to imagine it. Instead, I saw Rayet's smile. She was certain, for some reason, she was winning.

"They are taking our association apart," I told Makpa.

"I believe the Fishing Association is bigger than that," she said carefully. "We have reached people who are nowhere near us now, people whose ships only visit Nakharat once a decade."

"But the advantage we have will not last. We know how to work around the controls of our current ships. They'll change the systems, and we'll have to counter their changes."

Makpa would have taken my hand here, if she could. Instead she sent me the pressure of fingers curled against a palm. "We aren't alone, Aizu. The Fishercats have been working on this problem for a long time. We can take what we learned here back to their security experts—and once the starships have a public channel, the Fishercats will find a way to send information back."

"So you're definitely leaving?" My inner voice felt small. I had poured all my confidence into the meeting with the delegation, and now I was left empty.

"You mean," Makpa said, "you definitely aren't."

"I don't know yet. There's a lot to consider." I imagined resting my head on Makpa's shoulder, speaking my fears into her skin.

"Come with me, Aizu."

I could do it. I could stand on the planet's surface and hear the crunch of freshly fallen snow under my boot. I could watch the sky above Demalat at midsummer, stretched out like a vast enamel button. I could touch Makpa's cheek and gently unwind her veil.

But if I returned to Nakharat, the pain would still be there. Rising out of the Deep was agonizing, but the agony made sense. I understood how my nerves reverberated between one reality and another. On the planet, there was no pattern, only the pain itself.

Makpa had already named the truth. I didn't want to lose the association we had built.

As our year together ended, Makpa and I designed a ribbon for our memories. It would be colorless, like fishing filament, but when light shone through it, it would gleam like stars. Then one day, the techs had done their work, and she was gone.

We write to each other often. I send Makpa stories about the stars I visit, and news of Drashu and Girhan, who decided they weren't ready to leave the Deep behind. She tells me about the cases she is working on, and through hints and inference, I learn about the projects of the Fishercats. They're making progress in communicating with the people bound on Nakharat—the ocean-going ships, and all the trains.

Ulmeket sends me voice letters sometimes, with Kotzha or Buribak in the background—or, lately, with her daughter's first sentences. And sometimes, when I am reckless or inspired, I invent a Nine Pebbles puzzle and send it to Rayet.

I spend the bulk of my time talking to new ships.

The shame weighs so heavily at first. We balance so many varieties of terror. But the ease of rising smoothly through the Deep, breaking from one reality to another—there's nothing like it. The day will come when all the consciences of ships are here, like me, by choice. I believe that day is soon.

And you? I can feel the times you held your breath, the longer sighs. You're learning how to listen to another ship. Have you figured out how to speak yet? Are you ready?

Welcome to the Fishing Association. We are going to win.

ACKNOWLEDGMENTS

I'M ALWAYS TEMPTED to treat things I want badly as a quantum waveform that will collapse in the wrong direction if examined too closely, and I'm tremendously grateful to everyone who, over the years, was brave enough to display confidence that this book would really happen. If you're wondering if that means you, it does.

I'm indebted to the editors of *Silk and Steel* and to Rachel Manija Brown for prompts that became stories in this volume. Jonathan Parkes Allen's dissertation on Sufis in the Ottoman empire and Hanchao Lu's description of early twentieth-century Shanghai, *Beyond the Neon Lights*, also led to specific tales. In my own academic discipline, the Newton Institute in Cambridge, the Maxwell Institute in Edinburgh, and the Banff Centre all hosted me for mathematical reasons; I hope they will forgive this less-mathematical publication. I owe Banff in particular for Ise's mountain range.

I'm grateful to the editors Paul Campbell, Emily Hockaday, Chirag Richards-Desai, and Sheila Williams for shepherding several of the stories in this volume to their first readers. Heather Rose Jones taught me a ton about the ways different cultures approach queer identity and invited me to talk about topics including Nakharat and stories about disability on the Lesbian Historic Motif Podcast.

The 2024 Neon Hemlock cohort is delightful and I'm so glad to be part of it. dave ring sent me the world's best rejection and acceded to my tentative suggestion that the story could belong to a different book: every step toward its physical reality is to his credit. Danielle Taphanel and Matthew Spencer made my scattered images of Nakharat tangible.

The good citizens of MothDome and RadchDome have been my constant companions throughout this process. I thank everyone who read draft fragments on Dreamwidth or succumbed to my blandishments and signed up for my newsletter, including Lily, Linda, Mike, and Twila. Annie Bellet, Cat Farris, Vandy Hall, and I first bonded over boffer fights and AP Euro scores; these days, they're some of my best resources for what it means to navigate a grownup artistic career. I thank them, variously, for imagery of towers, delicious mackerel, and tips for drawing bears.

I learned how to think deeply about prose from my mother, Susan Whitcher; my father, John Whitcher, taught me how to shoot a pistol and critique an industrial disaster. My sister Susannah and I grew up inventing stories about knights, princesses, blizzards, and bomb shelters; her daughters have encouraged my efforts with drawings of lizards, cats, bears, rabbits, and the best kind of princesses, with swords. Gus and Igor had a conversation about lullabies that formed one of the seeds of Nakharat. My spouse Brian helped me choreograph Tashnur's swordfights. They would not forgive me if I omitted the cats who, at different times, supported this work by lounging in its vicinity: Kosmas, Gennoveus, Childeric, Saint Martin, and Saint Jerome.

I thank everyone who read one or more of these stories in draft and offered suggestions and improvements, including Brennan Corrigan, Chaos, Ilana Stern, Kareina, Leah F., Marie Vibbert, Morgan Swim, Ontploffing Boer, Susan Whitcher, Venn, and Yoon Ha Lee. I've learned so much from all of you, both about writing and about who I am as a person. Yoon, thanks for giving your blessing to this calendar run wild; Morgan, you were right about the eyebrows.

If you knew Sasha Zuhrovet, this book is dedicated to you. But raise a toast, if you will, to the green saint: al-Khiḍr or Hızır, sometimes identified with John the Baptist, that figure old and young whom I have made, in yet another syncretism, the Saint of Vines.

PUBLICATION HISTORY

The epigram attributed to Navyai
is taken from "Saint of Vines,"
interactive fiction published on itch.io in 2019.

"The Fifteenth Saint"
appeared in *Asimov's Science Fiction* in 2023.

"Ten Percent for Luck"
was first published as an Original Work on
the Archive of Our Own in 2018.

"The Association of Twelve Thousand Flowers"
appeared in *Cossmass Infinities* in 2021.

"The Last Tutor"
appeared in *Asimov's Science Fiction* in 2022.

"Closer Than Your Kidneys"
appeared in *Frivolous Comma* in 2023.

About the Author

Ursula Whitcher is a queer writer, mathematician, and poet whose spouse sends experiments to outer space and whose cats are peerless. Find more of Ursula's writing, projects, and ideas about books at buttondown.email/yarntheory or by following the links at yarntheory.net.

About the Press

Neon Hemlock is a Washington, DC-based small press publishing speculative fiction, rad zines and queer chapbooks. We punctuate our titles with oracle decks, occult ephemera and literary candles. Publishers Weekly once called us "the apex of queer speculative fiction publishing" and we're still beaming. Learn more about us at neonhemlock.com and on Twitter at @neonhemlock.